Deadly Trials

Deadly Trials

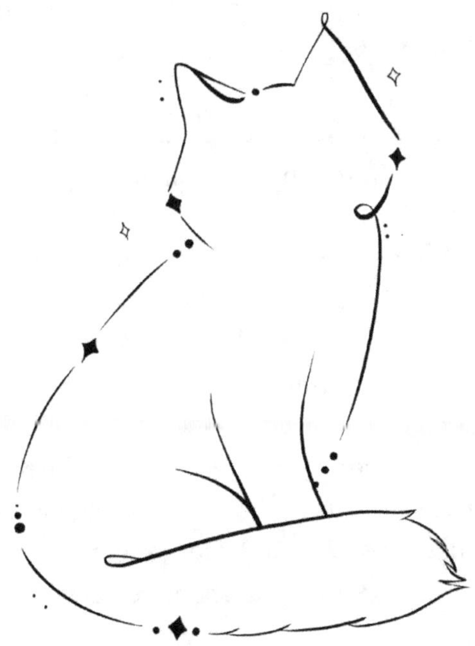

Lorelei R. Jensen

To my dearest Olivia,

This is because you threw a hissy fit because I dedicated Betsy last time. Just kidding.

I wouldn't have made it this far in life without you and your kind heart. I hope you save a ridiculous amount of lives as an EMT. Don't stop being friends with me now that you've gotten a book dedication.

To protect those who have mental health concerns, I am writing this page to warn you that there are a lot of triggers in this book. Please read at your discretion. There is depression, PTSD, domestic violence, emotional manipulation, and suicidal thoughts. These are serious topics and aren't portrayed in a joking manner. If you are struggling with any of these, please know you aren't alone and there are people who want to help.

Prologue

Screaming. All she could hear was the screaming. It rang in her ears, in her head, echoing through her body. Her soul quaked and body trembled. Her voice would've joined in the haunting chorus, but her jaw was clamped shut with a cold metal muzzle, so all she let out were little whimpers.

She would have ran if she could. If leather straps didn't bind her to the cold metal chair, she would have. Instead, she let her mind escape. Let it leave her body. Maybe it would find a safe place, somewhere warm, outside of the white room that had confined her for years and years. The wall was scratched from when she first arrived and marked the days she'd been stuck there. After months, counting became hopeless. Counting and hoping only brought disappointment, and set false expectations. At the beginning, she could've been saved. It was far too late now.

Her dark eyes followed a trail of dried blood to the one way mirror. She imagined all the people behind it, excitedly chattering over their new discovery. Ten more minutes until they released her from the confines of the chair and went to visit some other unfortunate soul, as they always did. They didn't even claim it to be science anymore. For them, all of this pain, all the death, the amount of suffering the experiments went through, was for personal gain and glory. The wall swung open, bouncing off the mirror with a loud bang.

"My darling niece," her uncle cooed. His arms were wide open in a friendly gesture, but the glistening syringe in his hand promised pain and suffering. "You won't believe what we accomplished today. You've been made perfect. You'll go down in history."

Curly brown hair stuck out in every direction, and his bloodshot eyes glimmered with excitement. His white lab coat fluttered as the air conditioning unit turned on.

He eased the needle into the vein in her arm, and liquid flushed into her bloodstream. Pulling the syringe out with a satisfied grin, he threw it into a stack of abandoned life support equipment. She tried to move her jaw, but the muzzle was too tight. So tight in fact that it cut into the skin of her neck and cheek. The discomfort kept her from biting her own tongue off. With no outlet of release, her anger bubbled uncontrollably in her throat: anger over the injustice, the pain, over her entire existence.

Her uncle's olive skin had paled over the years. Neither he nor his experiments had seen sunlight in months, if not years. The last time he went out, he dragged her with him. She forced the memories from her mind; if she thought too long about it, the churning in her stomach would turn into vomiting, and her heartache would overtake her.

Screaming in the room next to her cut off. The screams that grounded her to reality stopped, ringing in the emptiness of her mind.

Her uncle tucked a piece of hair behind her ear before pulling out a knife. He cut her arm, laughing maniacally. Whatever liquid he had injected into her was working; despite being cut over and over again, she didn't feel a thing, even her jaw stopped hurting. Panic clawed at her throat as blood ran down her arm and fingers. He'd cut the artery in her arm, causing her to bleed profusely, and each pulse squirted out more blood. Her head spun with the rapid blood loss, but the cold grasp of death was welcoming.

The wound closed up, reconnecting the sides of the artery cell by cell. Muscle and skin regenerated as seconds turned into minutes. No scars blemished her skin. Tears streamed down her face and blurred her vision.

A perfect weapon. He made her a perfect weapon.

He threw his head back in ecstatic laughter and danced around her chair. "Beautiful. I couldn't ask for a better niece. You'll help me save the world."

The hidden door behind her swung open, hit the wall, and revealed her small world to many disgustingly happy researchers. More footsteps followed after them.

Her uncle untied her. Once she had hit the ground, he replaced her leather bonds with handcuffs and a chain. With a hard yank on her arm, he made her stand and forced her to line up with ten other girls. He shook in his excitement, rattling her metal leash. His eyes leapt eagerly from one girl to another. Unlike her, the others were not muzzled. They all knew she'd do anything just for a chance to get out of there.

Her dearest friend, a plump, gorgeous redhead, nudged her arm and gave a small smile. Hope lit up her chocolate eyes. They were always filled with unfounded hope and positivity. That's why she could smile despite having her stunning looks used as a political maneuver. There were only hours left before this amazing friend would be given as a gift.

They were both beautiful and dangerous, just as the politicians wanted. Five girls were going as "gifts." They pretended someone would save them. All of the girls did, even the ones who wouldn't have to spend the rest of their miserable lives warming up some bigshot's bed. Maybe it comforted them, but she couldn't share that sentiment. She had convinced them to take part in her plan because of her lack of faith.

"3900631 has finally reached perfection. After six years, we've accomplished the impossible," her uncle explained in a warm and gentle tone. "We can now commence Operation Estrella."

Cheers filled the room as the scientists and researchers celebrated years of hard, dedicated work. The girls stood sober in their line. She looked at her best friend, trying to swallow the remnant of her tears.

With child-like excitement in his eyes, her despicable relative gestured towards the girl. "Anything you'd like to say at this world-changing moment?"

"Yes," one of her companions replied. Her friends spoke in unison, but she couldn't hear what they said. Her body knew though.

She wanted to scream, to speak, to ask why. Her mind fought her body as she raised her left hand in a stiff salute. The girls watched her, and their betrayal ripped her heart to shreds. Relief settled in their faces, and they relaxed, knowing what was coming next. They looked at her with great expectation as the researchers fled to the door at the opposite end of the room. Her uncle was dragged out by his men. Screams of terror filled the air as he sealed the researchers in with her.

Hope filled her friend's tear-filled eyes. "End this for us." The command rang clear in her mind, echoing over and over again as she lost full control of her body.

Chapter 1

Scrolling through the tablet she shared with the Kimura family, Leah deleted any pictures with her in the frame. She hesitated with each one, burying her unpleasant emotions deep within an overflowing box. For the past year and a half, Amyra Kimura and her son, Cassian, took care of her, practically adopting her into their family. Her gratitude was immense, but it was time for Leah to move on.

Warm light filtered through the open window in her bedroom. Leah sat on the wooden floor, leaning against the wall, and a small bag rested against her leg. A small bed with soft clean sheets and a wooden wardrobe decorated the room. Thin white curtains draped across the window and fluttered in the breeze. A blast of air caught Leah's hair, blowing pink strands in her face.

Continuing to swipe, a photo of the three of them appeared on the tablet. Amyra, a stout woman with chestnut curls and dark brown eyes, stood between a smiling Cassian and a brooding Leah. Leah didn't like to consider herself brooding, but looking at the picture, she found it hard to think otherwise. Cassian didn't seem to mind it though, which confused her.

The best way to describe him was tall and broad. Even for a Galorian, Cassian was tall, standing a head or two taller than his own people. He smiled often and laughed easily, which charmed many of the local townsfolk. Add in his fluffy chestnut hair and emerald green eyes, and few people could resist the eighteen year old. Leah being one of the few.

Leah fell a couple inches shorter than Amyra, but as half-Lirith, height was never going to be her best aspect. The photo had caught her fairy-esque form—small and thin, too thin. Her hair fell in thick pastel pink strands over her shoulder, and obsidian eyes pierced through the inanimate tablet, unsettling her present self. A black tattoo poked out underneath the collar of her shirt. Her skin finally gained a healthy color to it, like the desert sand in the afternoon sun.

Pressing delete on the last picture, Leah finished removing her existence in the Kimura's life. *It is for the best.* Emotions crept up her throat and it took a minute to swallow them down. *Keep it in. No emotions. Weakness gets you killed.*

She leaned her head back and waited—waited for a lot of things. She waited for this nightmare to end, waited for a stupid letter, and waited until the day she could see Alayna again.

I swear I'll save her.

Her stomach growled. Reluctantly, she pushed herself off the ground, grabbed her bag, and wandered out of the room. The door creaked loudly as she pushed it open, but the hallway was quiet for the late morning, too quiet. She remembered Amyra mentioning doing an errand run the previous night, but usually Amyra sent Cassian to do it.

Leah found Cassian's room empty. Strangely empty. His usual mess of adventuring gear was nowhere to be seen. Four incredibly full backpacks laid on his bed. The walls were bare save for a map of the Neforian

Abyss. Leah eyed the map warily. She needed to get there even if it cost her humanity.

She turned away and headed down the flight of stairs at the end of the hall. Taking them slowly, she examined the house one final time. As soon as her letter arrived, she would leave, and despite her better judgment, Leah wanted to ingrain every last inch of the house into her memories. She knew better, but this place had become special. She tried so hard to fight those feelings, locking them away in her box. They slipped out, though, and left a horrible feeling in her mind.

Leah reached the bottom of the stairs, sharply turned into the kitchen, and walked straight into Cassian. The window, wide open, showcased the open fields of the surface world. The scent of freshly cut grass and baking bread filled the small room.

His eyes widened and wandered to the fridge. Leah glared at him and rubbed her nose.

"Morning," he said. He bounced on his feet. With suspiciously quick movements, he made his way into the dining room.

Leah ignored him and headed to the fridge. As soon as she opened the door and searched for the pudding she'd bought the night before, it dawned on her. *That brat.* Slamming the stainless steel door shut, Leah turned to the sink and found the empty glass container. It had been washed and everything.

Leah stalked after Cassian, glass in hand. He sat at the round wooden dining room table. It was hand carved with years upon years of memories engraved in it. An arrangement of sunflowers, daisies, and lavender sat in the center of it.

With a loud thud, Leah slammed down the glass container and glared daggers at Cassian. A guilty look settled on his face. She huffed angrily before sitting across from him, eyes never leaving his face. He opened his mouth but snapped it closed.

He stared at her miserably. "I'm sorry, Leah. I thought it was Mom's," he gloomily said. Today, he wore extremely casual clothes, but it suited him. Grass stained the knees of his pants.

"That makes it better?" she asked, cocking her head and crossing her arms. Her lilting accent highlighted the wrong sounds, making her irritated. Despite speaking the language for two years, her Lirith accent still broke through with its singsong vowels.

He smiled sheepishly. "Well, no, but she doesn't usually mind." He rubbed the back of his neck. "I'll make you another one."

"There is no need." She got up. Forget leaving on bad terms, it would only make Cassian more annoying. "All is forgiven."

His shoulders slumped in relief, and he turned to stare outside the window. Cassian stood, peering closely through the glass. His face paled, and Leah followed his gaze down their dirt driveway. Amyra walked up the path with mail in her hand and a scowl on her face.

Leah and Cassian stared at each other. With a slight nod from Cassian, Leah whipped out of the chair. They had about a minute to get out of the dining room to somewhere safe. Amyra had explicitly banned them from entering the drawing for the Trials. Leah assumed she would get to her letter before Amyra got to the mail, but Cassian had snuck so many pictures of her and Amyra, that it took way longer to erase herself than she had expected. Cassian leaned against the window, keeping an eye out.

"Should we apologize?" asked Cassian. His warm voice shook.

"Remember last time?" Leah shivered from the memory. Amyra forced them to help Granny Linna, an elderly woman with a deep hate for the world, especially young people. They cleaned her house for hours, leaving only when the old lady deemed her dusty and cluttered house suitable. *How on earth did someone collect so much stuff?* "The thought of that mold makes me want to vomit."

Cassian rested his head on the wall. "Never again. I'd rather clean the graveyard at night."

"Even with Uncle Roger's ghost." Leah nodded in agreement.

Cassian whimpered. "Ghosts aren't real," he tried to convince himself.

"We could run to the store." Leah headed to the back door, past the kitchen, close to the late Weston Kimura's study. The door of the study was cracked open. Despite the man being gone for eight years, Cassian and Amyra couldn't bring themselves to touch the items in the room. Too many memories.

"And have her yell at us in public? No way," he shouted across the house.

She placed her hands on her hips, yelling back at him, "Do you have any suggestions?"

"I wouldn't be here if I did," said Cassian with a sigh. "She was going to find out. Might as well face it head on."

Leah opened the wooden back door. Cassian was such a wimp. "I need to live to see another day."

The afternoon sun blinded her. Her eyes adjusted to the light, leaving her gawking at the crowd. They were surrounded. Leah had no idea how Amyra gathered the townspeople so fast, but the whole town gathered around the house, blocking Leah's escape. Irritation flooded Leah's brain briefly as she examined the crowd.

Elric, a young man determined to woo Leah, stepped up. Grief was written all over his face. He liked Leah because she was pretty and quiet. He wore overalls and a dirty white shirt. His mouth flapped up and down as he tried to articulate his obvious disappointment in her.

"Leah, do ye think it's acceptable for a young girl like yourself to enter those darned Trials?" His tone was harsh and mocking. The crowd murmured their consent.

Leah leaned against the doorframe. "I am twenty years of age. It matters not whether you and your friends find it acceptable. I am neither related to you, nor a citizen of this country. I am free to do what I will."

Elric flushed an unbecoming red and stomped up to her. "What good do ye think ye can do? I bet ye never seen bloodshed in yer life. It's a man's world in the Trials."

The crowd backed up as Leah laughed mockingly and narrowed her eyes, sizing up the innocent young man in front of her. She pitied him and showed it on her face. His rather average face twisted in rage, his mouth a thin line, and nose scrunched up to his forehead.

"You are just jealous that I, a stranger in your territory, took one of the two places in this area." She spoke in a straightforward manner. He invaded her personal space and looked down on her. His wretched breath blew over her nose, and it took all of her self-control to refrain from gagging. She backed into the house, trying to avoid him. "Do not fear. I will be gone before you know it."

"You need to learn yer place."

Leah scoffed. "I need to learn my place? Elric, you need to learn where your place in society is, and at the moment, it is below mine a—what are you again? Oh yes, a mail carrier."

The crowd murmured. The elderly mayor, a short, balding man with a beer belly, stepped out of the masses. "Elric, you said there was an emergency. Did you call us because you're mildly inconvenienced over the fact that our dear Leah got into the Trials when you did not? Child, it's a draw, fate even." The mayor shook his head and beckoned for everyone to follow him. "

Elric breathed heavily and turned away. Leah rolled her eyes and cleared her throat. "You are a sad child, Elric, getting mad over someone taking your toy."

A loud clatter startled her, but she refused to turn around and acknowledge it.

"Mom," Cassian yelled from the front of the house. Panic overcame his usually calm voice. "Please put the pan down and think about this. Violence is not the answer."

A few of the townspeople turned by chance to see Elric swing at her. She moved her head out of the way. His fist was slow, and he didn't form it properly. The boy would break his thumb if he made contact with anything.

A vein popped out of his forehead. "Yer not even wanted here, so how can ye be so confident?"

She kicked him in the groin, and while he curled to protect his injury, he brought himself eye to eye with her. He paled and opened his mouth to speak, to beg. Only squeaks escaped his trembling lips. Her fist collided with his nose, breaking with the force of the hit. Elric screamed like a little girl.

Leah drowned in the noise, and panic ran up her spine. She lunged, pinning Elric to the ground, and brought the tip of her elbow down on his temple. His grey eyes went in and out of focus.

"Cassian!" a woman screamed, gaining Leah's unwanted attention. Screaming and yelling annoyed Leah more than anything else. It was more like all loud noises, especially thunder. Thunder was terrifyingly loud. The woman squeaked as Leah forced her eyes up at the woman.

Leah stood, keeping her body close to the ground in case someone came at her. The townspeople began to run. As they should. She didn't want to attack them, but they showed that they were in her way. It was easier to take care of them now than deal with them later. Leah had learned that the hard way.

Someone ran up behind her. She slipped her dagger out of its spot in her jacket's sleeve and twirled it at the attacker. The metal tip glistened in the sunlight and pressed against Cassian's neck. Neither Leah nor Cassian moved.

"What are all y'all doing at my house?" Amyra shouted with her hands on her hips. *So it wasn't Amrya.* Leah pondered for a moment, grip tightening on the worn handle of her blade. "You might be excited for the two of them, but it isn't acceptable to ambush them in our own home." Amyra let out a yelp, finding Elric's beat up body in front of her. "Leah!"

"He swung first," Leah mumbled, slipping her dagger back into its sheath. She grabbed Elric's collar and pulled him as high up as she could.

"Now tell me how you found out about my acceptance," Leah hissed in his ear. "Did you peek at the mail when you came to deliver it? Answer quickly or I will break your arm." She twisted it far behind his back until he started whining.

"Enough!" Amyra swung around. Anger creased her brow, and Leah trembled. "Just because he swung first doesn't mean you get to take him out! You shouldn't be surprised the whole village knows. The letters are easily recognizable. Now, go bring him inside and patch him up," Amyra said, forcing herself to take a deep breath. Her fingers traveled up her face, resting on her temples which she rubbed, fighting a headache. "Actually, let Cassian do it. I fear you'd only cause more harm."

Elric whimpered when Cassian and Leah slung his arms around their shoulders, though Leah hardly helped. She was too short to actually do anything. She grumbled and kicked up dirt, stalking into the house.

Chapter 2

Leah watched from the window in Wesson's study at Amyra apologizing to the neighbors, and they began to disperse. A few turned back and looked into the window, making eye contact with Leah, who met their gazes with a cold indifference. Amyra's face was as red as a tomato, and Leah couldn't tell if it was anger or embarrassment, but most likely both.

The late Wesson Kimura was an orderly man with a kind smile. Pictures of rare artifacts, magnificent places, and family portraits decorated one wall of the study with a label accompanying each photo. A display case filled with mysterious objects lined the wall by the door, and shelves upon shelves of books and notebooks covered the rest of the wall. Under the window sat a large oak desk which Leah perched on.

The view from his desk was calming. Open fields of golden grass and a plain that stretched as far as her eyes could see met the sky like a shore touching the waves. Light peeked through gray clouds, leaving shadows that darkened patches of grass.

A picture of the three of them was buried in a desk drawer. Cassian inherited his height, green eyes, and kindness from his father. His call for adventure also came from the man. This love brought him fame, as Wesson brought more objects back from the abyss than anyone else. His party of talented men and women were legends now. He traveled further into the Neforian Abyss, explored the most ruins and cities, and documented much more than any adventurer before him. On his travels, Wesson died a painful, tragic death, leaving his ten year old son and his beautiful wife alone in a world that had suddenly become much darker and lonelier. The day he and all his friends died was unforgettable, but at least he didn't die alone.

Thousands of people had died, trying to find fame and wealth in the Neforian Abyss, a place of unimaginable wonders, magical treasures, new discoveries, and life-changing secrets. It was quite common since many dangerous creatures and poisonous plants lived in the different sectors, or levels, of the abyss. Those things didn't matter to Leah. She was not interested in the thrill, though she wasn't sure she could even feel those types of emotions. Money and fame didn't matter to her either, and knowledge scared her, or the thirst for it. No, Leah had something waiting in the abyss for her, someone waiting for her.

Leah hobbled over to one of the bookshelves, grabbing one of the many notebooks Wesson had written throughout his journeys. It was filled with illustrations of the many beasts he encountered and notes on strange flora. Detailed maps marked ruins and escape paths as well as areas to avoid. The paper was yellowed, and Leah felt the writing through the paper.

She placed it back on the shelf, brushing off the piling dust onto the floor as she grabbed another volume. Leafing through the pages, Leah connected with the man who'd written such elaborate notes on the six sectors he traveled through before meeting his untimely demise. Both the surface world and the first three sectors, the Hinora Sectors, mourned his death.

Non-Neforian born people were only allowed to live in the first three sectors. That's where she and Cassian would live if they got immigration passes, but Leah needed more access, which is why the whole town was upset. Few people in each county of the surface world obtained permission to even test for the adventurer's license, which gave a person exclusive access to certain places, specifically countries bound by the Treaty of the Righteous, top secret information, and the Guild Hall, which was the best place for an adventurer to find jobs.

Cassian had won one of the Trial positions, and Leah got the other. They applied behind Amyra's back, which was one of the reasons she was angry. They didn't even plan for it to be that way. The only reason why Cassian knew Leah got in was because she had left her phone wide open when he came into her room a few weeks ago. The Trials were one of two ways to get into Neforia. The other was to pay your way, and it was a hefty amount. Very few people survived the Trials, and they only happened once a year in each of the four surface countries.

The door creaked, and Leah whipped around. Cassian slunk in, the light in his eyes faded from the scolding his mother had given him. He sat in his father's desk chair and leaned his head on the wood, taking in long breaths.

"I thought I'd find you here. Mom wants you. It's going to be bad," said Cassian with the enthusiasm of a rock. "She also wants you to apologize to Elric."

Leah's face scrunched in disgust. "I would rather be decapitated."

"Be careful what you wish for. Mom might just do that." He laughed and gave her the worst reassuring smile.

She calmed her emotions, burying deep within her box. Leah could apologize if there was no anger or irritation. With light steps, she steeled herself for the inevitable scolding she'd get. Not that she didn't deserve it. Things got out of hand because of her lack of self-restraint and emotional control. *How did they learn about it anyway? I did not tell a soul, and the letters looked like normal mail.*

As soon as Leah left, Cassian opened one of the desk drawers. His hand lingered on the cold brass knob. Taking a deep breath, he pulled out the letters from his father. A photo fluttered out of the stack onto the ground by his feet.

He bent down to pick it up. Tears welled in his eyes. It was the last picture with his dad. The three of them—Amyra, Cassian, and Wesson—had stood in front of their old house, a large three story home with bay windows and a porch. Amyra had wrapped her arms around Wesson, who kissed her forehead. Cassian had stood between them with a huge grin, barely coming to his dad's chest.

He swallowed the lump down.

After the photographer had taken their family pictures, Wesson and Amyra took Cassian on a picnic. They walked forever and Cassian had grown so tired, but the exhaustion faded away immediately at the sight of his dad's favorite place in the world. It was past their tiny town, deep in the woods. Birds called overhead and little animals scurried at their feet. His dad brought Cassian to a small glade. It was picture perfect. They had eaten and chatted for so long. Cassian never wanted to leave.

He wished he could go back to that time.

It was that day when Wesson told Cassian and Amyra that he was going deep into the abyss with his party and an acquaintance. They were to find Katharnia, a legendary place with an ancient and powerful source of energy that could save the world. But it was only a legend, and his dad never came home.

Cassian hadn't cried the day when his father's acquaintance brought the news. He didn't cry at the funeral. His mother needed support, so he kept the pain hidden, but both physical and emotional wounds festered when not addressed, and he wasn't sure how long he could continue ignoring it before it ruined him. Finding and caring for Leah eased the hurt and slowed the decaying of his heart.

Cassian placed the photograph on the desk and sighed, rubbing his hand on his face. The pain never went away. A hole ached in his heart from being torn away from his dad. Wesson Kimura didn't die by drowning. It wasn't until recently that he figured that out. Pages of his notebooks were missing and artifacts that were documented in his dad's notes were nowhere to be found. Wesson Kimura was murdered, and Cassian would do anything to find out the truth. Not that the call of the abyss was not tempting. As a child, the abyss was his goal, and he needed to go there to bring himself and his mother peace.

With a rekindled determination, he pushed himself out of the chair. He strutted to the door as Leah opened it. The large piece of wood smacked into his skull, causing him to stumble backwards. Leah froze before rushing to his side. It was moments like this where Cassian thought he saw her true personality. Behind the huge iron wall she built around her emotions and past, Leah was really caring. Painfully caring, but she hardened herself so much that few people saw anything but indifference and dislike.

"Your mother said we are to pack our belongings," Leah said after releasing Cassian from her worried grasp. "She would like to leave before the evening."

"Thanks for checking on my head." He said with a huge smile. "I'm already packed so I'm going to hang in my room. Want to join me?"

Leah considered for a moment before nodding. "I shall."

"Most people say will instead of shall." He held out a lemon drop. After many weeks, he figured out those were her favorite candies. "Good attempt, though. You're grammatically correct, but not going to lie, it sounds pretty stuck up."

Leah grumbled at him, saying something in Lirithian, and took the candy. Fuming, she popped the lemon drop in her mouth. Cassian held the door open for her, and she stomped out. He took a final look around his dad's study. *This is probably the last time. I really need to take it in.* His breath hitched, but he rolled his shoulders back. This was for his dad.

The kitchen smelled amazing, but while Cassian was hungry, he heard Amyra sniffling. He bit his lip hard enough for it to split, keeping the tears from running down his face. He ran upstairs. Leah laid on the rug in his room. She sat up at the sound of his sniffling.

Cassian turned away. "Sorry. This is pretty embarrassing."

"You are allowed to mourn, Cassian." She stood up and walked over to him. He looked at her with his face full of tears. He sucked in through his nose, choking a little on snot. She stared up at him with her head at an odd angle. "Change, while inevitable, is painful. Leaving those behind is painful. You have emotions and must use them." She gave a smile that failed to reach her eyes. "Do not worry. Your mother is strong and well loved by the town."

He wiped his face on his sleeve. "You act wise in the worst scenarios. Now I can't stop crying."

"Then continue to cry." Leah looked at him, but her eyes were distant. "Some people cannot cry, no matter how painful the experience."

Chapter 3

A curtain fluttered out the open window. The moon hung high in the sky, illuminating three figures running on a roof. The marble balcony glistened in the moonlight. Besides the faint chirping of crickets and the occasional "who" from an owl, the night was silent. One of the figures slipped into the magnificent marble mansion through the carelessly opened window. The wealthy should know not to leave themselves open and vulnerable. The other two figures sat on the roof, keeping watch, or pretending to.

Aeron sauntered into the home of his latest victim. Gold adorned every wall, paintings and vases worth more than Aeron sat in plain view, and three guards roamed the hall with confidence. He let his smile grow, holding back a laugh. The mission was too easy.

Sneaking in the shadows behind the closest guard, a lean man wearing all black, Aeron sliced open the man's jugular. The guard gurgled, choking on his own blood and alerting the other guards: a female (nicknamed Flight by Aeron) and a bulky male (Bulks). The man slumped to the ground, and while Aeron's opponents were momentarily distracted, he pulled out his gun.

Aeron pulled out a handgun, aiming it right at Flight's head. He pulled the trigger and released a bullet straight into her forehead. The crack echoed around the room, ringing in the halls. She couldn't have dodged if she wanted to. The thrill he'd been waiting all night for finally arrived as adrenaline rushed through his veins.

Bulks jumped in from behind Flight and swung at Aeron. An alarm sounded, and Aeron noticed the two shadowy figures on the roof—his older, but useless siblings—run off. In his irritation, he let loose on Bulks. Shot after shot rang until he emptied his magazine. Bulks fell to the ground with shock riddled on his face. Aeron slipped in his second magazine. He only brought two, which was his mistake, but he wouldn't need another one. His confidence outweighed the worry.

His siblings' jealousy fueled his ego. But after a while, even Aeron got annoyed by their pettiness and lack of thought. What he really wanted to do was end them like some of his victims, while they begged and pleaded in a disgusting manner. Instead, they scurried away in the shadows like rats that were caught with a flashlight.

Aeron enjoyed the rush of a kill, and thrived within the adrenaline. It was better than the hours of mundane lessons and other boring events he had to attend. Anything was more enjoyable than sitting with the crazy hag that called herself his mother.

Why did being heir have so many responsibilities? Aeron wanted to have a good time, nothing else.

Gunshots rung. A hole appeared next to his head. Dust and marble particles landed on his pristinely pressed black suit. He sighed dramatically, swinging around to face his new target, a newbie who shook in his boots. The suit was a few hours old, a gift he bought for himself as congratulations for having a successful mission the night before. Otherwise, their last words would distract him, and he'd inevitably get punished.

"How're you going to pay for this?" Aeron asked. His deep voice echoed, and the trembling of the young man satisfied him. The man took off running.

Reinforcements piled in, and Aeron smiled as his adrenaline powered him on. He shot one dead, while injuring the leg of another. Ducking under the arm of an assailant, he pulled the trigger and killed the newly injured one. Shot after shot, men fell.

Until all that was left was Aeron. The final man tumbled onto Aeron before hitting the ground with a loud thud.

He tugged at his shirt, stained red with blood. A piece of white hair fell into his eyes. Many found his lilac eyes beautiful. His victims found them cruel and terrifying. They promised them a death that would be memorable even in the afterlife. Their predatory gaze sunk deep into the memories of any survivor. Aeron rarely let his prey escape though, so those lucky few lived in fear. He enjoyed the chase more than the hunt, but the kill truly satisfied him.

With the confidence of a king, he strutted down the hall into the master bedroom, throwing the large double doors open. The room was like most rich politicians': open floor plan, a sofa, random golden objects, and a huge bed. A fat old man squealed like a startled pig at the sight of the strikingly beautiful, yet bloodied young man. Aeron smirked. The old man buried his head in the fluffy white comforter on his four poster bed.

"Don't kill me," the man cried.

Aeron gleefully ripped the comforter off the bed. Ugly tears streamed down the elderly guy's face. "Is it money? I'll pay you more than they offered. I'll triple it even. I'll even give you my daughter and house; please don't kill me."

Throwing his head back, Aeron laughed, and it echoed alongside the sobs. A crazed look settled in his eyes. One bullet left in the magazine, and one bullet left for an unwanted pig. Aeron pulled the trigger, and with the bullet flying right into the skull of his target, blood soaked the sheets, spreading throughout the white.

"This is boring," Aeron whined. *They always say the same things. I want a fight, an adventure. Something.*

A crumpled up newspaper fluttered to the ground. Aeron picked it up. As he glanced through it, a smirk settled on his lips.

"Now *this* could be good."

Chapter 4

How was this hidden for so long? Sebastian flipped to the beginning of the book he'd been reading, an in-depth study of genetic mutation written by Doctor Alajandro Perez. Looking at his phone, Sebastian gawked at the time. *Five thirty in the morning. Again.* He really needed to stop staying up so late, but his studies weren't going to finish themselves.

Knuckles rapped violently against the front door. Banging on the door early in the morning was never a good sign. Usually it means bad things happened at a bad time so people were sleep deprived. Sleep deprivation causes anger and irrational behavior. Sebastian knew this from personal experience. Silas, his twin, tended to be sleep deprived.

Shaking, he got off his desk chair and headed to the front door. His mother was already there, opening up their home to their visitor. Her black hair was braided in dozens of braids, a common hairstyle amongst the village women. Acceptance of whatever news would be given softened her expression, but her jaw was clenched in anticipation. Chidinma, his youngest sister, crept up behind him, clinging onto his arm. She looked up at him with her golden eyes, sharing the same fear as him. *Did something happen to dad?*

Silas stood at the door with his girlfriend's father, Lethabo. Anger burned in his eyes as Lethabo shoved him to the floor. With a thud, Silas' knees hit the gravel in front of their doorway. He whipped around glaring at the man.

Fingers tightly gripped at Sebastian's other arm as Oluchi, Chidnima's twin, joined them. Her kind silver eyes were similar to their mother's, but they were stricken with the same fear Sebastian now had.

"Yer son informed me that my daughter was raped by his brotha," Lethabo said angrily to their mother. Sebastian couldn't blame him, but he'd never touched a girl like that, especially not his brother's girlfriend. Which could only mean one thing…

The man pointed an angry finger at Sebastian. "Come 'ere, Son. Yer aboutta meet yer maker."

Sebastian attempted to back up, but failed as his sisters' grips were too strong. Not because they wanted to keep him there, but because the two girls were afraid. It had been a few years since Silas had his last run in with someone's father.

"I beg your pardon," Sebastian's mother said. Her silver eyes narrowed, and the man flinched. Their mother was one of the village's best warriors, protecting the autonomy of the village from the surrounding country of Quenza. She had the pride of her people. Indignation straightened her back. "My son did what?"

"Yer son touched my baby girl."

She pointed to Sebastian. The morning light glistened off her ebony skin from the rising sun. "This one here?"

"Yes for the Lord's sake, Ms. Nia. That's what the good one said." Lethabo huffed. His fist dangled at his side, and Lethabo trembled.

Sebastian trembled too. Fear clawed at his throat and stomach. With as much courage as he could gather, he forced himself to make eye contact with his twin. Silas's expression was amused, a twinkle in his eyes and a smile lit up his face. *I should've known.*

Silas wasn't a bad guy per say. He just had bad tendencies. Nia and their father believed it came from the summer they had separated Silas and Sebastian. Sebastian left for the city for a medical training program, and Silas spent it on the farm with their uncle.

"It wasn't me," Sebastian protested, mustering up all of his courage. He flinched when Lethabo moved towards him, but Nia moved to block him.

Silas laughed. "Don't listen to 'im. We all know, he's a liar."

Rage boiled in Sebastian's stomach from all the false accusations. There was nothing to be done. Silas won. He won every time, and Sebastian was going to have to pay for Silas's mistakes again. Silas committed a crime. Silas committed a crime, and Sebastian was going to be beaten again, maybe worse.

With a shrug, he separated himself from his sisters. Oluchi whimpered, trying to get her grip back on him. Chidinma held onto her twin, tears spilling from her golden eyes. He patted their heads. "Go to my room and lock the door. Mom will get you when this is over."

"Brother," Chidinma started, clinging to her twin.

Sebastian gave her a shaky grin and wiped a cheer off her cheek. "It'll be alright. Your big brother promises. Now, head into my room."

"We're no longer children, Brother," said Oluchi. Her voice filled with emotion.

"I know, but Mother can't keep Mr. Lethabo back much longer." He looked over his shoulder. The two were screaming at each other with a fiery passion. "Do it for me."

With great reluctance, Oluchi and Chidinma hurried to his room. It wouldn't keep them safe, but it was the furthest room in the house. They wouldn't have to hear what inevitably would happen next.

Lethabo pushed Nia aside and stomped into their house. He grabbed Sebastian by the neck with the force of a full grown elephant and slammed Sebastian into the wall. Air rushed out of his lungs.

"The Council's already decided, Boy. I can get me way with ya. Yer gone. If yer alive when I'm done with ya, yer bum better be outta here." Lethabo let go of Sebastian. Sebastian fell to the ground and tried to crawl away. An elbow dropped onto his back.

He crouched into a ball and covered his head with his arms. One hit after another, Sebastian endured. His hands slipped, exposing his face, and Lethabo took the opportunity to kick Sebastian until he could no longer open his eyes.

Nia grabbed onto Lethabo, trying to stop him. It was to no avail. With a little bit of hope, Sebastian peaked out of his swollen eye. Silas leaned against the doorframe. His smile was wide as he watched. Nia hit the floor, shaking from the force of her sobs.

The truth was, Nia could be punished for fighting Lethabo as the council gave him the authority to punish Sebastian as he pleased. They could do nothing so Sebastian closed his eyes. It would at least allow for his image of his beautiful and strong mother to be preserved. He wanted her presence to continue to be a strength for him if Lethabo killed him.

Darkness surrounded his consciousness, and not the being-knocked-out kind of darkness. No, the kind that kept him up at night wondering why he even bothered waking up every morning. The kind that makes him wonder if all this was worth it. Night after night, day after day, Sebastian wondered. As Lethabo slowed down, Sebastian hoped it was the true end.

A cool sensation washed over his face, easing the pain. "Brother?" Chidinma whispered. It sounded so close, and yet so far like a dream. *Did I protect them well enough?* "You're alive? Right? Please answer me."

Sebastian struggled to sit up, and Chidinma moved the ice pack away. Pain rippled through his body. Bruises formed on his ribs, arms, face, legs, stomach. Bruises formed everywhere. He was hurt, but he'd survived. He must've passed out because Lethabo was long gone, and his mother was in the kitchen, calling their father.

Silas laughed. "What a fool. Couldn' even get the right twin."

"Do you think this is funny? Does it make you happy when you see Brother Sebastian in pain?" Oluchi raised her voice. She tried to step around Sebastian, but both him and Chidinma kept her back.

Silas scrunched his nose up, and he narrowed his eyes; his lips became a thin line, stretching out the scar on his right cheek. He stalked up to the three of them, and reached over Sebastian's head to grab Oluchi's face. "You're pretty stupid goin' against me."

"The only reason you can act like this is because Dad's not home." She wrenched her face from his hand, moving as far away from him as possible.

Silas made for Chidinma, but Sebastian grabbed his arm. Taking all the attention of the teenaged girls, Sebastian glared at Silas. His heart raced in his chest from the act of defiance, but he had to protect his sisters.

"Silas, don't take it out on them. They're just kids," said Sebastian with a steadier voice than what was actually going on in his head. *He's just in a bad mood. Silas always gets a little angrier when he's up late. He still loves us.*

A dark fist rammed into Sebastian's eye, pummeling the bruise. The injury flared up. He whimpered, too afraid to let out any noise. Silas wrapped his hand around the back of Sebastian's neck. "Did I give ya permission to speak to me like that?" He slammed Sebastian's head into the ground. It went pitch black again.

"Brother!" Chidinma screamed.

"Mom!" Oluchi cried. "Mom, you've got to stop Silas."

"Don't think I won't hitcha too," Silas growled. Oluchi let out a yelp, and footsteps followed.

Sebastian forced himself to grab Silas's arm, despite his fear and his pain. He trembled violently and sweat dripped down his dark skin. "I'm sorry. I'll be better next time. You're an awesome and kind brother. All you do is love us, and I was disrespectful. I'm sorry. It was my fault. It always is, so please leave them out of it. I swear, I won't speak to you like that again."

Silas calmed as Sebastian predicted he would. Trying to get his heartbeat under control, Sebastian took deep breaths. His sides ached, but nothing hurt more than the betrayal of his brother. Time after time again, Silas left Sebastian to clean up his messes, but Sebastian couldn't escape. He didn't even know why. Something always brought him back.

Is it because we're mirror twins? Are we attached by some sort of genetic bond? I hope that isn't the case, but after reading about the mind control that they can perform through genetic manipulation, I'm thinking it may be a possibility.

Silas and Sebastian were perfect reflections of each other, looks-wise.

They had the same nose and similar physiques, but what made them different—even though everyone still mixed them up—was the mirroring of their facial features. Sebastian had a golden left eye and silver right, and Silas had the opposite. They even had matching scars on their faces. It had happened when Sebastian got glasses for his fading eyesight. The fear of being separated caused Silas to slice open their cheeks. That was after Silas attempted to kill Sebastian over the glasses.

Chidinma and Oluchi joined their mother in the kitchen. Within minutes, Nia walked out into the room by herself. Face twisted in rage, and fingers wrapped around her spear. "Silas, I have failed to raise you properly. I'm giving you an hour to pack your things and leave." Her voice echoed.

Their personalities were like day and night. While his twin chose violence and lust, Sebastian made vows to never purposely harm another lifeform. It was a sacred vow to him. One made in order to be a doctor. Silas wanted power, and when their father was gone, he ruled the house with fear. Both Nia and their father were out for most of the week. Their father mined and Nia guarded the village and other surrounding areas. Silas kept Sebastian, Oluchi, and Chidinma shackled, and Sebastian couldn't do anything.

Silas didn't appreciate being told to leave. He lunged at their mother, but Sebastian was weak. Too weak. He could barely raise a finger. A hand grabbed Silas's shirt collar, choking him like a wild dog on a leash. Silas whipped his hand back, smacking his assailant across the face.

Their father stood as straight as a board. His father's golden eyes hardened, glistening like precious metal. With the shaft of her spear, Nia smacked Silas's legs from underneath him. He fell to his knees.

Sebastian could hear his father's teeth grinding. From his anger, a vein popped out of his forehead.

"Pack your bags, son." His deep and rich voice rumbled in the silence.

Silas stood up and brushed off his knees, losing against their dad. Their father left him absolutely no choice. He'd have to leave, or face the consequences of the village. Silas scratched the back of his neck, scowled at Sebastian, and stalked up stairs. His door slammed shut.

Calloused hands pulled Sebastian from the ground into a warm hug. Tears leaked from his eyes onto his dad's grimy shirt. The scent of sweat and the mine shaft, while disgusting, comforted Sebastian.

"I tried to convince the council, but they refused to listen," his father said. Emotions choked his words. "You'll have to go, son, and your brother is going to force you along with him."

Nia wrapped her arms around them. "This'll be hard for you, but I pulled some strings and got you accepted into the Trials. Lady Elizabeth was a mentor of mine. I was planning on sending Silas and another villager out, but it seems you'll both have to attend." She kissed his cheek.

"I can't—" Sebastian cried. *I'll break my vows. He'll make me.*

"We know, but you might find people who can separate you." Nia patted his head. "Silas doesn't have to be your world anymore."

His father shifted to welcome Oluchi and Chidinma into their embrace. The two were crying and pulling on Sebastian. "You'll keep your vows. We know you will." Oluchi handed him a good luck charm, her good luck charm, a thin silver chain with a ring dangling from it. It was her treasure from their grandmother.

Sebastian wished the warmth of the moment could last forever, but wishes rarely came true for anyone, let alone him. He had no choice but to let go, and that hurt the worst out of all of his injuries.

Chapter 5

The quiet snores which escaped from Leah's lips startled Cassian. *Leah sleeps? I mean, I knew she had to.* Leah's impenetrable walls made it impossible for her to show weakness in front of anyone. She was always awake when he'd gone to check on her in the past. Even now, despite her sleeping in front of someone, her back was to the wall, and she faced the door. Cassian refrained from getting too close to her in fear of facing the dagger in her sleeve. He sat on the floor at the opposite side of his room. Some of her fears had calmed from when she was first found half-dead in the alleyway.

With a quiet knock, Amyra entered Cassian's room. She eyed Leah before sitting on the edge of Cassian's bed, examining the empty room. Tears ran down her cheeks. "I'm so very upset at you two."

He avoided her gaze. "I'm sorry. I really am."

"If you were truly sorry, you'd unpack your bags and throw away that darned invitation!" She startled Leah who awoke and hit her head on the wall.

Seething in pain, Leah got up and moved to the carpet by Cassian's bed. She sat down with a humph and rubbed her eyes, fighting the remnants of sleep. "I am not sure what is happening."

"We're getting scolded," Cassian said. Amyra sniffled.

"Again?" She glared at him like it was his fault. "I already apologized to Elric." She shivered at the memory. Elric lorded over anyone who he thought was lesser than him which included the prideful Leah. "I will never get caught beating him up again."

Amyra huffed over Cassian's laugh. Elric deserved what he got in Cassian's opinion. Not that he had been there for what happened, but because Elric deserved any act of violence after what he said to Leah when they first met.

"You should be reflecting on your behavior, Young Lady. That's why I grounded you from pudding." Amyra's face reddened. "On top of your violent behavior, you two had the audacity to go behind my back and sign up for those—those horrid Trials."

Leah sighed and flopped onto the carpet. "Did you wonder if it was because we knew you would act like this that we refrained from telling you?" Amyra gasped.

"Leah!" Cassian threw the closest object by him at her, irritation building up. She rolled out of the shoes way, rolling right onto the hardwood floor. "You better treat Mom with respect."

"Apologies," she mumbled to the floor. "I am just disturbed by my lack of pudding today. I would be able to suffer the punishment if someone had refrained from eating mine."

Cassian grumbled. Leah looked at him from a weird position. Her head was at an odd angle, and she gave him a smile. It was a rare occurrence, like seeing a double rainbow on a sunny day. *She's having a blast at Mom's expense.*

Leah stood up abruptly, surprising Amyra and Cassian. She rushed to the window, and her expression turned blank. With a loud crash, a rock flew through the window. Glass flew at her face, cutting her face.

With a handkerchief in hand, Amyra ran to her side. Blood dripped down her cheek for a mere moment before the skin patched itself back together. Cassian's stomach squirmed.

He joined them at the window. Three hours after he'd been publicly beaten, Elric and his goonies were back for more. Leah whispered in Lirithian and opened the window. It didn't click with him what she was doing until she stepped onto the sill. He grabbed her shirt as she jumped, but gravity pulled the two of them down. Amyra screamed for them as they landed on the bushes outside their house.

Leah popped up from her two story fall. With animal-like reflexes, she chased after Elric. His goonies caught the wild look in her eyes and sped off. Cassian brushed himself off, already aching from the fall. Bushes were not as cushioning as he once thought they'd be.

A large bang alerted him of Amyra's entrance. "Leah Kimura! If you beat that boy, I will personally see you don't get on the train tomorrow."

The threat worked, and Leah stopped in her tracks. She held a large rock in her hand. Amyra strutted up to Leah, grabbed the rock, and made her way to Elric who stood by the tree at the edge of their property. Cassian and Leah followed after her. Nerves ate at him. Amyra grabbed Elric by the ear and began walking down the hill to the town. He screamed and cussed her out, earning a rock to the back from Leah.

"I thought Leah had been extreme when she beat you, and the only reason why she got away with only an apology was 'cause you tried to hit her first." Amyra twisted Elric's ear, and the young man yowled like a dog. She picked up her pace. "We're going to the police station. I'm filing a complaint."

"If you'd reigned in that—" Elric broke out into a cry.

"Leah isn't one to be controlled. You've got no right to try to oppress her either."

Leah stopped at the edge of the hill, sitting on the dirt path. Cassian sat beside her and watched as Amyra scolded Elric.

"Your mother is strong." Leah's expression was hard to read.

Cassian nodded. "She's really upset with us."

Birds chirped in the afternoon light as the two of them sat there, waiting. A breeze caught up Leah's hair, blowing it into Cassian's face. Cassian laughed as she tried to tame the long strands. After a long time of sitting in silence, Leah stood up and walked towards the house. His back ached as he trotted to catch up with her.

When she got to the door, Leah turned and faced Cassian. Her brows were furrowed. "I forgot to mention this earlier, but you should be careful about what you say when you are in the Trials. You never know who is listening."

What does she mean? Cassian stood outside pondering her words. He was pulled out of his thoughts. He forgot to buy his train ticket!

Chapter 6

Weaving through the throng of people, Aeron made his way through the train station. It had taken forever to get from the capital city of the Kapain nation to the dingy town in Galor, and he was tired, hungry, and bored. Aeron hated traveling.

He blended in well in the crowd without too much presence. The only thing sticking out from everyone else was the shock of white hair on the top of his head, and maybe his outfit. After spending a ridiculous amount of time in front of the mirror, he picked a simple outfit of a black dress shirt, matching slacks, and a leather jacket.

A few ladies watched him as he passed by, but that was as much attention as he was going to get. He smirked at one of them when they walked next to him briefly, crinkling the corner of his lilac eyes. She blushed, turning away to hide her giggle. Aeron was satisfied by the brief moment of entertainment before boredom sunk back in.

With some excitement, he openly admired the new technology of the magnet train. Its sleek white form created beautiful aerodynamics. However, a girl with pink hair stood in front of his view. Her body was tense, and she held herself more like a soldier than a civilian. Her posture was incredibly straight. With trained eyes, she surveyed the station. Aeron glared at the back of her head. As if she could sense his stare, she whipped around.

The expression on her pretty face said anger, but the set of her lips and the dead look in her eyes conveyed indifference. She was with an older woman and a guy around Aeron's age. An unfriendly hand gesture accompanied her unfounded dislike for him. Aeron returned the gesture with a smirk. *This is one of the weirdest encounters I've had.*

Her male companion turned to look at her, saw the gesture, glanced up at Aeron, and paled. He grabbed the girl's face and scolded her, which only earned Aeron another glare.

The woman grabbed the girl's ear who accepted the punishment with a great reluctance, and dragged her over to Aeron. The boy followed awkwardly behind them. His face red with embarrassment. In most cases, Aeron would've left before any form of confrontation, but curiosity got the best of him.

The three companions stood before him. The boy and the older woman were obviously mother and son. A lingering sorrow burdened her shoulders, but the burden didn't hide her motherly presence. They had similar facial features and hair. Instead of being intimidated by the boy's towering height, Aeron was reminded of a big loyal dog. He could practically see a tail wagging behind him. The boy and girl gave off couple vibes from their matching outfits. They wore black long sleeve shirts and khaki pants. But while the girl wore combat boots and a black cardigan, the boy wore sneakers and a brown vest.

"I'm so sorry about my sister," the boy said. "She didn't mean to be rude. Right, Leah?"

The girl scoffed and looked over her shoulder, keeping a vigilant eye for suspicious behavior. "We are not siblings. I am only a freeloader at your home."

Aeron shook his head and held back a shiver. *That would be a disgusting couple. Siblings are a no. Why would they wear matching outfits? They didn't even look related, but who knows. Maybe, there was an affair.*

The woman whacked Leah in the back of the head. Aeron laughed at the look of absolute disdain she gave the woman.

"You better apologize, young lady." The woman's voice was so warm and affectionate that Aeron had to do a double take. *Was she being fake or was she always like that?* From the crease in her brow, Aeron detected concern, but was it for him who may have been offended, or Leah who seemed to have something off about her?

Ire flashed briefly across Leah's face. Aeron almost missed it because it came and went so fast. The others missed it, but they most likely didn't get the same intensive training as he did. Very rarely did non-clan members have the opportunity to learn such body language. Aeron smirked. He was going to have fun with this one.

Leah stared intently at him. Her dark eyes pierced straight to his soul. Recognition lit up her eyes, and the corner of her mouth lifted up before she realized he was staring at her. Aeron strode up to her and invaded her personal bubble. He leaned down to talk to her, striking a nerve. She stared up at him with a lot of attitude.

The boy watched their interaction with great intensity, and his mom stared at her phone, pulling up her virtual tickets. She glanced up nervously.

"I'd be really grateful if you'd let me come with you guys. This is my first time traveling alone." He traveled a lot, but this would be more interesting. With the presence of a sheltered, rich kid, Aeron lied.

The boy flung an arm around his shoulder, grinning like it was the best day of his life. "We'd be happy to have you with us. I'm Cassian by the way."

"Aeron."

Leah grimaced. "Cassian, you do not invite strangers to travel with us. It could be dangerous." She glanced pointedly at Aeron, and he rolled his eyes.

"It'll do us no harm, Leah," his mother said. "I'm Amyra."

With her mouth hanging open, she began to protest. "You do not kn—" Leah froze, staring off behind him.

Aeron followed her gaze to find a middle-aged gentleman walking towards the train. He was a typical Quenzan with thick brown hair and dark eyes with even darked bags under them. Large glasses framed his eye bags. Leah tensed up and her eyes narrowed, never leaving her target. She flexed her hand as if she imagined a knife or sword in it. Cassian flicked her forehead. A move Aeron would have hesitated to make. *You never distract a cornered beast.* To his surprise, she loosened up and calmed the bloodlust. It wasn't completely gone though. One wrong move would blow her over the edge.

Amyra watched with fear in her eyes, but Cassian and Leah acted as if nothing happened. *Interesting.* Cassian casually leaned over and whispered in Leah's ear. Aeron assumed that he meant to be quiet.

"Put the knife away," Cassian scolded quietly, trying not to drag attention. Aeron barely heard it over the crowd that was gathering to enter the train. Amyra joined the masses.

Aeron couldn't tell if Leah listened, but he was entertained. *These two are a mystery.* He hoped they relieved his everlasting boredom. If not, they'd meet a quick demise. No one would know it was him either.

"I look forward to traveling with you." A dangerous smile settled on his lips.

Running into Aeron Sefic was an unpleasant experience for Leah, similar to when Amyra found her in the alleyway. Luckily, neither Aeron nor the Kimura family recognized her. She glared at the back of the heads of the three ignorant beings before making her way towards the train. Few could imagine the shock she felt when she realized she made it all the way to Wesson's house in her escape. Lost in thought, Leah rammed into Cassian's back.

"Apologizes," she muttered, stepping around him into the train. Cold air slammed against her face as the train's air conditioner pushed out as much air as possible.

"No worries," he said, following after her. "Just pay attention inside the train. It's super packed."

People had forced themselves into the very front, pushing each other out of the way for the premium seats. Leah saw glimpses of the red carpet underneath her feet. Too many heads blocked her view of the rest of the rows, and she was squished between Aeron's back and Cassian's chest. Putting her hands on his jacket, Leah used Aeron to bulldoze the crowd.

"Not to be that person, but using me to plow through the crowd is quite rude," Aeron yelled over the angry crowd. "If you knew who I was—"

"I would continue to do the same thing. Now, move to the back," said Leah as Cassian placed a hand on her shoulder. Behind him, Amyra held onto his arm, fighting to stay close.

Aeron shook his head, but did as he was told, weaving his way through the crowd and pushing people who stopped in the middle of the aisle. They were nearing the end of this particular train car when he came to an abrupt stop. An irritated Leah peeked around him, letting out a groan.

A young woman with curly red hair and vibrant green eyes gawked at Aeron. When Leah looked up at his expression, it shocked her. A boy so arrogant should've been happy by the obvious admiration. Aeron smiled at the woman, but his eyes gleamed dangerously like a provoked beast.

Cassian's grip tightened around Leah's shoulder—a warning. She slid in front of Aeron, dragging Cassian with her. A weird squeak sounded from the back of his throat.

"You are in the way," said Leah sharply. Only the end of the sentence had a lilting vowel.

"Aren't you rude?" The woman glared, sizing Leah up.

"Very." Leah shoved past. "It seems your parents never told you how rude it was to stop and stare. What a pity."

Cassian smacked the top of Leah's head. She whipped around with her hands covering the now throbbing spot. "I'm sorry. What she was trying to say was she'd like to go around you. She's not from around here."

Leah stared at Aeron from around Cassian and rolled her eyes. He let out a chuckle, earning a glare from the woman. Leah almost smiled, but swallowed it down. It was scary how similar he was to Mel. She would have been around his age if she were still alive.

Looking past Aeron, Leah met eyes with a glowering Amyra. Quickly, Leah turned back around to the fuming young woman.

"You're asking me to forgive her because 'it was lost in translation?' Absolutely not. You're a terrible liar, sir." The woman flipped a piece of hair out of her face. "Do you even know who I am? I'm the daughter of Abaddon Sefic."

Leah snorted, causing the woman to redden in the face. A crowd was gathering around them. She should've felt bad for starting a fight. Amyra always told her she should, but Leah was in a sour disposition. Being around both Aeron Sefic and Cassian Kimura drove her mad. Memories of days long forgotten by them resurfaced in her mind, putting her in the foulest of moods. Long held anger and resentment bubbled to the surface, not at the boys, but at the situations around their first encounters. In the pettiest way, Leah wanted everyone else to be as miserable as her.

"You? A Sefic?" asked Leah. She let out a loud, cruel laugh. "That is hilarious. In what ways would you be able to resemble a Sefic?"

The woman stuttered. "How would you know the difference?"

Pulling on an arm, Leah brought Aeron forward. He was laughing, while Cassian and Amyra were getting ready to give Leah the scolding of a lifetime. Again. "Well, first of all, if you look at my Sefic example, you would see that his eyes are a light purple, specifically lilac. From what I have heard, that is a gene that ninety percent of the head's children have."

Some of the people pushed past them, not interested in a petty argument between girls. The crowd wasn't there for them, but to get out of the completely filled car which Leah and the others now blocked.

The woman reached for her own eyes, looked at Aeron, and paled. "I'm so sorry."

However, Leah was not done. An apology wouldn't cull her pettiness. She yanked Aeron's sleeve up his arm, leaving a red mark for the shirt was too tight to be pulled like that. Exposing the underside of his forearm where he was branded. A shadowy bird standing on two knives was burned in his skin amongst hundreds of little scars. Aeron's eyes widened like saucers. "How do you know?" He paused for a moment to think. "Actually, keep your secrets. I wanna find out on my own. It's more interesting this way."

"Do not speak," Leah said to him. "It is annoying."

"You're using me to prove a point. I should at least have the privilege of talking."

Cassian grabbed Leah's ear, forcing her to let go of Aeron. She clamped her mouth shut to avoid making any noises. His eyes were narrowed in irritation, and a shiver ran down her spine when their eyes met. She looked away from him.

"I am truly sorry for this one. She's lost all social skills from being in an orphanage for so long. I'm also very sorry for lying to you. Please take this to make up for the trouble we've caused." Cassian handed the woman a few coins. She shook her head and shoved past Aeron, running to where her companion was. He yelled at her, but her frantic look and actions instilled fear.

Leah struggled out of Cassian's pinch. Her ear throbbed. "I knew she wanted our money."

"I kinda figured. Weird that she used the Sefic name though. We're not that well known," said Aeron, backing away from Amyra who was stalking towards Leah.

"A news story came out a few weeks ago about some fool who killed a wealthy man under the Sefic's name." Leah turned to escape from Amyra's wrath, but Cassian caught the back of her shirt. "This is quite unfair. I do not deserve this treatment twice this week. They both deserved it."

"The woman didn't do anything, and Elric would've been handled by someone else." Cassian growled. He handed Leah over to Amyra. She fought to escape until the two of them had calmed down. "Come on, Aeron. I believe the train is heading out in the next few minutes."

With furrowed brows, Leah stood next to Amyra. Aeron looked over his shoulder and laughed at Leah's pursued lips and narrowed eyes. He swung open the door to the next car.

"What's going to happen to her?" asked Aeron as the door closed behind him.

Leah didn't hear Cassian's answer, but Aeron laughed loud enough that she could hear him through the door.

Chapter 7

Sebastian wanted to go home. He missed his parents and worried about Oluchi and Chidinma. He wanted to go back to school and study late into the night, but weeks had passed, and he still hadn't escaped from Silas. Hours and hours, the two of them had sat in the car. His back ached. In Silas's mind, traveling in a car was much cheaper and more efficient than crossing through three countries in the train system that connected the whole surface world. The trains were significantly faster than the old automobile Silas had found, and cheaper since gas prices had shot up thanks to the countries in the abyss holding back their reserves.

Despite the long distance they needed to travel, Silas refused to let Sebastian drive which meant that Silas was driving eighteen hours a day without sleeping. Sebastian hated to admit how scared he was over the situation. After much arguing and almost getting slapped, Sebastian finally convinced Silas to stop in an incredibly sketchy town, with one very run down motel where Sebastian currently sat on one of the rickety twin-sized beds.

The room had only been thirty honders, and the quality of the room reflected its price. Bars blocked the windows closest to Sebastian's bed, and a metal screen covered the glass. A mysterious red stain lingered in the dirty off white carpet. He tried not to imagine what it came from. A tiny bathroom was by the door of their room. On top of the toilet barely working and needing to be replaced, the sink had very little water pressure, making it nearly impossible to wash his hands.

Sebastian shivered. He wanted to go home so bad, but it wasn't like he could abandon Silas and go home. The village wouldn't welcome him back until the misunderstanding was cleared. Tears threatened to fall, but he forced them down. If Silas woke up because of the noise, Sebastian would be in big trouble; though he was amazed that Silas hadn't woken himself up with all of his snoring.

His stomach growled as boredom sunk in, but Silas had thrown away his textbooks two weeks ago when they began the journey to the capital of Kapai. Sebastian had been extremely disappointed when Silas had gotten a hold of the report about Professor Perez's escaped experiment, his own relative. It was a true mystery how one man could come up with such a world-changing experiment and not get discovered. Sebastian was disgusted with what he did to those humans—those girls.

The boredom grew greater, and Sebastian peeked at the ugly green door which was just past Silas's bed. As long as he was back before Silas woke up, he'd be fine. Taking a deep breath and grabbing his backpack, Sebastian strengthened his resolve and took the first shaky step. The second step was much easier; the third and fourth were barely an inconvenience. His hand gripped the cold handle, and with one final look back, he opened the door. His heart pounded as it creaked loudly, but Silas snored away without being disturbed.

Dirty, worn carpet lined the dim hallway. There were many ugly green doors with profanities and threats scrapped into their paint. A few of the lights flickered like in those horror films. Sebastian shivered and hurried away as fast as he could without looking weird. Housekeeping passed him as he made his way to the motel's entrance, and they looked like they did more than just cleaning houses. At least the motel's entrance had lots of windows, filtering in natural light. Relief from the sight of the doors filled him.

Sebastian nodded at the stewardess behind the counter, and practically bounded out into the open, heading straight to the convenience store he'd seen on the drive to the motel. A dust devil kicked up the dirt around him. The sun warmed his skin pleasantly, and he couldn't help whistling all the way to the store. It was only a few blocks away from the motel, but the sense of freedom he felt was almost overwhelming. He wasn't sure what to do with the new feeling, but he decided to enjoy it.

The convenience store was the most disgusting building Sebastian had ever laid eyes on. Bird poop covered the ground all the way up to the glass doors, and so much gum darkened the sidewalk. A bike gang drove away as he tiptoed—trying to avoid the dirty ground—into the air conditioned building. He was relieved to see them go.

The greasy haired employee greeted him with the enthusiasm of a rock, which disappointed Sebastian, but didn't surprise him. This area was known for being poorly managed, with many gangs and criminal organizations. Maybe he should've stayed in the room after all.

No! I made it this far. I might as well get something to eat.

To his delight, they had a slightly wilted salad without any meat. Something about eating animals didn't settle well with him, so he tried his best to avoid eating them. He walked over to the glass fridge. There were so many fingerprints and food and drink splatters he could hardly see through the door. Touching the metal door handle as little as possible, Sebastian grabbed a green tea, rushing to the checkout counter.

A gunshot cracked right outside, followed by an elderly woman screaming for help. She was tall and thin and carried herself with the air of a queen. White hair piled loosely on the top of her hair. Her eyes were turning red from crying, and she looked around frantically. Sebastian ran out the door as the attendant hid behind the counter. The woman fought to catch her breath and speak as tears streamed down her face. "My—my husband," she said through gasps. "My husband needs help. They've shot him."

Sebastian looked around, but there was no one in sight besides the old woman. His heart raced, and a cold sweat seeped through the skin on his hands. He took a deep breath. *The more nervous I am, the worse it will be for the patient. Breathe. You'll be okay, Sebastian. Everything will be okay.* Peeking his head back into the store, he said, "Call an ambulance."

Leaning against a blue SUV, her husband tried to keep his calm. Sebastian rushed to his side. Blood soaked through the man's shirt, and his breath was ragged. He stared at Sebastian with sea green eyes. His wife crouched beside her husband, holding his hand. The bullet had gone straight into his abdomen.

"I'm going to attempt to help you until an ambulance arrives," said Sebastian as he pulled off his backpack. He searched for his tools, pulling out a pair of trauma shears and some gauze. "I'm not even going to attempt to remove the bullet. I'd do more harm than good. However, we need to make sure your clothes don't get caught up in your drying blood." He explained as he disinfected his hands and tools.

Sebastian wanted the man to be as comfortable as possible when the paramedics arrived. Being as careful as he could, he began cutting off the area around the entry wound. After the area was exposed, he used gauze and placed pressure on the wound.

"I know you're in a lot of pain, but emergency services will be here soon." Sebastian needed to keep the man awake.

"I will hardly die from human mechanisms. I was just caught off guard," the man replied angrily.

From the length of the man's legs, Sebastian recognized that the old man was tall. Incredibly tall. His salt and peppered hair was long and well kept despite the state that he was in. Sun weathered his skin, making him look like a sailor, but without the calluses on his hands. With narrowed eyes, Sebastian scrutinized the man—partly looking for any other signs of injury, while also trying to figure out his lifestyle.

"You are a fool, Eisointh." His wife cried. "The human child is genuinely concerned for you."

Human? Sebastian tried to keep his face passive, but Eisointh caught onto his curious expression. More and more people gathered around them from the surrounding stores and buildings. Eisointh's wife shooed them away so there'd be enough room for the paramedics. Sebastian admired her authoritative presence. A siren sounded close by, coming nearer by the second.

"We are of the dragon's kin." The elderly man laughed as Sebastian's jaw dropped. His jovial noise made the older man yelp in pain. "I should really be careful like Vaytylth said, but it is nice to see that not only my wife is worried about me. I have met few humans such as yourself."

The ambulance passed by the motel, speeding over to the convenience store parking lot, and the crowd made way for it. It pulled to a quick stop; three men and a short woman hopped out of the vehicle and raced over to Eisointh and Sebastian.

"Sir, we'll be getting you to the hospital real soon." The woman took Sebastian's place and gave him a warm smile. "I'll take it from here."

"Can you tell me what you did?" the one of the paramedics asked as the other personnel put Eisointh onto a stretcher.

Sebastian looked around before realizing he was talking to him. "I removed a bit of his clothes around the wound and placed pressure to staunch the bleeding. I didn't give any pain medicine as I assumed you'd handle that."

His eyebrows rose into his hair. "Wow. I'm impressed. You've handled the situation well."

Sebastian smiled awkwardly at the praise. "I just did what I could."

"Which is more than most people can. You did a really good job, so just accept my praise already."

"Alright." Sebastian laughed. With a nod, the paramedic ran off to help Eisointh into the ambulance, and Sebastian was sad to see him go. His kind words, no matter how much flatter they were, warmed his heart.

Vaytylth walked up to him, pulling his dark hands into her pale and veiny grasp. With a kind smile, she squeezed his fingers tightly and a dark shadow swirled down her arm, brushed against his fingers, and struck like a snake into his skin. The shadow burned into a swirling tattoo on his forearm. On his wrist, a dragon head formed with flames licking out onto his hand.

Sebastian was scared. He brought trembling fingers up to his scar.

If Silas saw it, if Silas even thought he saw it, pain would be etched once again to the both of them. Sebastian swallowed back tears.

"You have been kind to us, and our kin never forget kindness." Vaytylth moved his hand from his cheek and cupped his cheek. "In your times of need, our people will help you and your people. Though it seems you have yet to find them, but do not fear, child. I see hope in your future, so do not give up just yet."

Sebastian opened his mouth. He wanted to know where her confidence came from, how she could promise such things to him, but she was gone. Everyone was gone like it had all been a dream. He stood alone in the convenience store's parking lot. He looked around, and determined it couldn't have been a dream. The SUV that the man had rested against was still there, and tire marks from the ambulance led away from the scene, *but where was everyone?*

With a grumbling stomach, Sebastian returned to the motel. He walked slowly, enjoying what few moments of peace he had left. The sun was setting. Bright reds and oranges reflected off the surrounding areas. Silas was going to be so upset with Sebastian, and he felt horrible about leaving him for so long. Taking one long reluctant look back, he stepped inside the motel.

Sprinting down the hall, he reached their room, and snuck in as quietly as he could. The door squeaked loudly, but it didn't matter. Silas had been waiting for him.

Silas punched him in the face, and he hit the floor. The air fled Sebastian's lungs. "Where'd ya go?"

"I'm sorry. I was hungry and wanted some food." He trembled. "It won't happen again. I swear."

Silas kicked Sebastian in the side. "It won't? I'm tired of hearin' yer excuses. I 'ave told ya time and time again, but ya don't listen, do ya? Ya coulda gotten hurt," Silas said, stomping on Sebastian's hand.

He cried out in pain, curling up to protect himself. *How much longer do I have to wait?* "I'm twenty-three years old."

"And ya think that makes a difference? Does bein' an adult maker yer disobedience a good thing?" Silas grabbed Sebastain by the collar and dragged him to eye level. "Yer my best friend and brotha. Everythin' I do is to keep ya safe. All ya got to do is listen."

Sebastian didn't mean for the look to slip. He truly didn't, but Silas wouldn't have taken that for an answer. Maybe the walls were thin enough for someone to hear and save him. At the very least, Silas hadn't seen the mark from the dragon kin.

Chapter 8

Trees flew past the window as Leah and the others traveled deep into Kapai. Night settled into the sky with the moon illuminating the landscape that flew by. As the golden hills painted silver passed from her sight, Leah concentrated on burying all residual emotions down. They always hindered her, and she thought she had been getting better at controlling them.

Amyra snoozed on Leah's aching shoulder, and despite her attempts, she couldn't get the lady off without waking her. She had no interest in speaking to the woman right now. It had been three days since she got publicly scolded, but Leah hadn't quite gotten over it yet. She now realized she was in the wrong, which was an improvement in Amyra's eyes.

With a screech of dismay, Aeron startled Leah out of her thoughts. He tugged out his earrings and handed them to Cassian who placed them in a pile behind him. Three stud earrings, one dangly cross earring, one black ring, his jacket, and a silver bracelet rested in the pile. The two boys faced each other; Aeron stared over his cards at Cassian, the dealer.

Aeron only needed to get over Cassian's 19 to win all of his stuff back. Leah watched with more fascination than she cared to admit.

"Give me another card," Aeron said. The card flipped over, bringing him over 21. With an exasperated sigh, he dug through his pockets, throwing stray cash at Cassian. Aeron deserved a little bit of losing in his life.

Leah had also learned the hard way when it came to gambling with Cassian. The guy's luck was incredibly high. After watching all the town's people lose to him, she began to think innocent little Cassian may be a cheater.

"At this point, I just want my stuff back," Aeron whined.

Cassian laughed, tucking the cash in his pocket. "I warned you. Gambling is not a healthy habit to have."

"Then why are you so good at it?"

Cassian smiled. "What fun would that be if you knew my secret?"

Aeron leaned his head back on the chair. "It's not about fun anymore. You've sucked me dry."

Cassian tucked all of Aeron's stuff into his backpack with absolutely no intention of giving it back. The train screeched as they approached the train station. The city's neon lights brightened up the night sky. Cassian's eyes were glued out the window.

"It's not that interesting," said Aeron.

"Cassian has never traveled very far from his home." Leah shook Amyra off her shoulder. "Those who make permanent homes in the surface area rarely travel."

Aeron eyed Cassian and his bag. "He doesn't act like a typical surface dweller."

"You two know I can hear you, right?" Cassian glared at them over his shoulder, breaking into laughter as Aeron glared back. "My dad was one of the greatest adventurer's alive. He taught me most of what I know."

Leah almost missed a flicker of intense grief, or something similar, in Cassian's eyes. He gave her a warm smile, and she considered it perhaps a fluke, but it was Cassian. He would never show his mom something like that, or would he? He was very sensitive to his and other people's emotions.

Passengers stood and wandered around the car as the train slowed to a stop. The attendants ushered them to sit until it came to a complete stop, but mankind was impatient and selfish. It had always been this way, and would continue to be, until all humans were destroyed. Human selfishness ruined everything. Passengers pushed past each other, racing to be the first one to the door. Some side eyed Leah and the others while they waited. Amyra, fully awake, chattered with Aeron and Cassian. The doors swooshed open, and people tumbled out, rushing to whatever destination waited for them.

After what felt like an eternity, Leah stepped on the platform. Racing thoughts overwhelmed her mind as hundreds of voices merged into one booming presence in her ears. Neon lights flashed everywhere, and people brushed past her, rubbing their skin and clothes against her own. Her heart thundered in her chest until she grasped all of those unpleasant feelings into her box.

Was it fear? I cannot be afraid. After years of fear and trepidation, she fought to keep herself uncanningly disinterested in her emotions and the lives of others.

Warm fingers wrapped around her cold ones. Cassian squeezed her hand. *It's going to be okay,* he mouthed. With a new strength, Leah took a step out of the way. The first step helped with the next as she joined up with Amyra and Aeron.

"You three need to find where you're going. I believe it starts tomorrow morning. Hopefully, they'll let you guys get some sleep." Tears rolled down Amyra's cheeks, and she crushed Leah in a hug. She stiffened, heart pounding in her chest. "I'll be watching, so you better come back."

Amyra took her warmth away. She refused to go any further with them. Something about Cassian and Leah needing to grow up at some point. Leah was relieved. Not that she wasn't grateful for all Amyra did for her, but it was time for Leah to let go of the Kimura family. Aeron met her eyes and smirked. A shiver ran down her spine as he turned and got a hug from Amyra. His face flushed a deep red. Something about him screamed danger. All Sefics should be handled with caution, but Aeron had something more going on with him. Leah had to watch for him. It would be best to kill him before he became a problem, but the crowd was too large, and she would need to lose Cassian.

Leah scooted away from Amyra and Cassian. Looking around, she felt as if she was being watched. There were at least a hundred people making their way out of the station. Tired children screamed and squealed. Conversations echoed off the walls. Despite all of the distractions, she pinpointed her target. A familiar face squinted in her direction before turning around and walking out of the station.

She bolted. Keeping her eyes on him, Leah ran up the stairs into the city. Cassian and Aeron shouted for her. A blond-haired man ducked into an alleyway. His locks swept perfectly across his forehead as he glanced his ocean blue eyes over his shoulder. He dressed unusually well, meaning he came straight from work. His eyes were wide with shock before he turned away, shaking his head ruefully. Leah looked behind her briefly, spotting Aeron and Cassian. Felix must've been reminded of Mel.

Weaving through the crowds, she cornered him in the alleyway. He hadn't noticed her yet. She slipped her dagger from her sleeve into her hand. Pressing the blade into his back, she smiled. "I have two questions for you."

Felix stiffened and broke into laughter. "Well, it all depends on the amount you're offering."

Leah let the man turn around and place her in a headlock. She accidentally laughed as he ruffled her hair. For a moment, she relished in her friend's presence. His disguise shimmered briefly. "You have grown. What a pity."

He let go, and his lips flattened against his face. "That's the first thing you say to me after going missing for a year? Jin-Ae, that's unacceptable."

"I tried to contact you, but heard nothing back. I assumed it had been you ignoring me this entire time." Cassian and Aeron ran into the alleyway. She flourished her hand. "Felix, this is Aeron Sefic and Cassian Kimura. This is Felix."

Cassian cocked an eyebrow. "Nice to meet you?"

"The pleasure is mine," Felix said with a polite smile, stretching out his hand. Cassian shook it amiably. "I'm Felix, Jin-Ae's best friend and longtime companion."

Leah gave him a side-eye. "You are not my best friend nor my companion. We are merely close acquaintances."

"Best friends." With his guard down, he turned to Aeron and Cassian. "It's nice to see her hanging out with people her age that are alive. Thanks for taking care of her."

"Jin-Ae?" asked Aeron. He leaned against one of the buildings.

A cold breeze wooshed through the alleyway, leaving Leah shivering. She forced all emotion out of her throat. "It is my birth name. Nothing more than a distant memory."

"Enough chatter. You're on your way to the Trials, right? I just happen to know where it's located. An amazing coincidence, isn't it? Not only did I get to see my best friend branch out, but we also are heading in the same direction." Felix laced his fingers in between Leah's. As always, he was uncomfortably warm.

With the confidence of a king and the footsteps of an elephant, he dragged her out of the alleyway. Not quite walking, but also not running, Felix weaved through the night's masses.

Stepping back into the world overwhelmed Leah. The bright lights from passing vehicles and from the cellular devices of the people walking around them, blurred together as she hurried away.

Cassian trotted behind her barely keeping up with her as he absorbed his surroundings. At one point, he stopped in Aeron's path. With a friendly whack from the assassin, Cassian focused back on the task at hand, following Felix.

Foreigners from all over the surface world gathered to watch the Trials. Because of the influx of foreigners, the city was beyond overpopulated. Some prayed their loved ones would make it through with only injuries. Others came to be entertained by the pain, suffering, and failure of those who participated. It was broadcasted worldwide and could be streamed on most platforms. It was a sport, entertainment that risked a life that wasn't their own. The past decade of Trials were available to watch like some cruel reality television show. Leah watched one of them, and the contents made her queasy.

The crowds thinned as they got closer to the edge of town, and Felix slowed down to an amble walk. Dawn crept over the horizon. Reds, blues, and yellows colored the sky. A few clouds were painted in vibrant colors. A bird flew overhead, singing its morning greeting. Felix squeezed her fingers and settled next to her, walking in-sync. Behind them, Cassian laughed loudly, head thrown back and arms wrapped around his waist. They left the city behind them, but one lone building, abandoned and probably filled with squatters, was in sight ahead of them.

"That's the building over there," said Felix. "It's much nicer on the inside, I swear."

It was peaceful, too peaceful. Peace only meant that something was on the verge of being destroyed. Peace concerned her. Leah was relieved when the young boy ran up to her, knife in hand. He trembled. A set of numbers, 3009312, were tattooed on his collarbone, and scars traced up and down his dark skin.

"Those numbers..." Leah yanked aggressively on Felix's arm. Her bottom lip trembled. "I thought you were keeping an eye on him."

Felix refused to look her in the eyes. "About that—"

Aeron ran up behind them, catching sight of the boy. He barreled past Leah and Felix, and grabbed the boy by the arm. The boy swung his blade at Aeron. "What's up with this rat?"

"About what?" Cassian popped in. His jaw dropped when he caught sight of Aeron holding the child up by the arm. "Aeron, that's not how you handle children."

"I've got no business with any men. I was just told to tell the lady that 'he found them.' Come on. Let me go." The boy wiggled.

Cassian snatched the child away from Aeron and carried him a distance away. Aeron watched with cold eyes, but stayed where he was. His lips pursed up in a pout. Meeting Leah's gaze, Felix began to inch away.

"Felix," said Leah in a monotonous voice. "I remember asking only one thing of you."

"I moved them. It's going to be okay."

Picking up a stone, Leah planned her assault. Aeron smirked as she invaded Felix's personal space. She switched from Galorian to Lirithian. Her voice rose with each word. "Okay. Okay? What about this situation is going to be okay? You promised."

Felix backed into Cassian who jumped in surprise. "Leah?"

Leah stopped in her tracks and held her breath. Emotions gripped at her throat, her mind, her body. They tore through her system. She hurriedly shoved them deep in her box, but they spilled out faster than she could force them in. Her throat closed up, and her lungs seized. *I can't do this anymore.* Her left hand gripped her ear.

"Jin-Ae, they're safe. I promise." Felix said in Lirithian. His blue eyes filled with concern. "They're in my country, protected by my best men. You can focus on Alayna."

Cassian gently grabbed Leah's arm, separating her from Felix. She flinched. *Again. Every time. I fail every time. Not much longer. I can hold on for a little, right? Right?*

Felix laughed nervously with his brows furrowed. "We're almost there, so why don't we head out?"

Aeron eyed her; a smile played on his lips. Cassian let her go, walking next to her.

"Aren't you a mystery?" Aeron whispered. She barely heard him through the noises in her head.

Without even sparing him a glance, she walked past him. "Mind your own business."

"And if I don't?"

Leading the others, Leah hurried over to the squatter building. Aeron followed closely behind her. "And if I don't?" He repeated with an irritating edge to his voice.

Swinging open the door to reveal a metal staircase, Leah walked into the building. "I will kill you."

Aeron scoffed. "You think *you* can kill me? What a joke."

"I see your fatal flaw is arrogance." A cruel smile slipped onto her lips. Her voice echoed off the walls, ringing in her own ears. "Lucky me."

Chapter 9

With the horrible stench of body odor wafting up the stairwell, Cassian questioned his life choices. Maybe he should've stayed home. He shook his head, pushing away all the negative thoughts. This was for his dad. He took a deep breath, and instantly regretted it. The smell was too much.

Their footsteps echoed loudly on the metal stairs, alerting the other unsavory Trial Runners of their arrival. Felix had left them as soon as they'd entered the building. He had something he needed to do and would be seeing them later. Leah led them into the stainless steel room where men and women of all lifestyles gathered around a stage. Cassian danced between a group of middle aged men who looked as if they had a more violent background. Their eyes were bloodshot, and tattoos of inappropriate designs covered the scars that riddled their bodies. One of the men got in his face, and he froze in fear. Leah and Aeron pulled his arms.

"Stick close," said Leah, releasing him.

Aeron let go and wandered next to Leah. "So what was up with that kid?"

She glared at Aeron. "Hurry up, Cassian. I am on the smaller size, so I need to be close to the stage."

He pushed through the crowd to walk alongside Leah. Not that he'd lose either Leah or Aeron; they stood out like sore thumbs. Leah's long pink hair popped out amongst the dull colors of everyone's outfits, and Aeron sauntered around like he owned the place.

"Ignoring *me* is a crime," Aeron said with a drawl. The look of utter disdain on Leah's face made Cassian laugh.

A snake-like man with lilac eyes and coppery red hair stopped in front of them. He scrutinized the three of them with an arrogant expression. Cassian was a bit confused by the silent confrontation, but Leah and Aeron ignored the man, trying to sidestep him.

"Little Brother—" the man hissed. "How'd you convince Mother to let you out? I assumed her favorite would be locked up forever."

This is awkward... Cassian stepped aside, trying to gauge the situation. He didn't need to step into someone else's family problems, but this interaction was incredibly hostile. Aeron stood straighter, and his presence was much more authoritative and less him.

Aeron smirked, but something flashed in his eyes. "I let myself out. Watch what you say, Brother Than. I've got no qualms reminding you of your place. It would be fun."

Than backed off a bit, taking a few glorious steps back. Despite his submissive actions, Leah stood in front of Cassian, blocking him from the situation as best as she could. Anger burned in Than's eyes as he looked at Aeron's calm expression.

"I see you've made some... What are they called again? Oh yes, friends." The man scoffed and dropped his gaze to Leah. All of the arrogance left his voice. "What are you doing here?"

Aeron's smirk dropped. "Do you know each other?"

"You don't remember her? She whooped your—"

"That is confidential information, and if you speak any more about it, I will have to remove you." She stood like a soldier: back straight with her arms resting straight down her sides. No emotions crossed Leah's face, and it startled Cassian. "It is a pleasure to see you again, Lord Than."

"It's not a pleasure." Than growled. Cassian agreed. This meeting was anything but pleasurable.

Leah shrugged. "Let us go, Cassian. It is best we do not involve ourselves in a long term family feud."

Following after her, Cassian realized there was much more to Leah than being a runaway. He should've known. There were so many signs, but encountering people of her past helped it click in his mind. Leah was more than what she had told him and his mother. However, Cassian's pondering had to wait until later.

"So why do you know Aeron's family so well?" Cassian whispered, looking around to make sure no one was listening. He knew Leah wouldn't answer otherwise.

Leah turned around and looked him dead in the eyes. "One day, you will learn of these things because it is inevitable, and no matter how much I try my secrets are always being exposed. However, for as long as I can, I will keep them to myself. Do not question me, and do not expect true answers from anyone we come across."

She made her way to the front of the empty stage and sat against it. Cassian moved to join her when he heard a loud crash. Than was on the ground with Aeron stepping on his head. Some reckless fool decided to join in, earning a knife through their throat.

Cassian wasn't sure what to do. Leah and the crowd made no intention of moving. Everyone watched with the eyes of uninterested predators. They would feast on the injured, but wouldn't hunt the healthy. Cassian stood disgusted by the disinterest in another person's life. He searched for someone who shared his pain, and he met his eyes. The man was almost crying, but he wasn't moving. He couldn't as if he was glued to the side of his twin.

"When did an illegitimate child get to talk back to the heir? When, Than? I must've missed something since I left the main house." Aeron put more pressure on Than's head.

Cassian took a deep breath, taking a risky move, and grabbed Aeron's arm. The cold blade Aeron had was pressed against his neck. A little blood dripped down Cassian's throat, and he was scared to breathe.

"You should stop," said Cassian.

Aeron smirked. "Why should I? You don't know me well enough to tell me what to do. As of three days ago, we were merely strangers."

Cassian gulped. "Come on. We should get going."

To his surprise, Aeron backed off. Not without one last step on Than's face, but he listened, and Cassian had no idea why. He was so relieved until Aeron began rummaging through his backpack. He grabbed a chocolate bar from it with Leah's name written on the foil. He trotted over to Leah.

"This chocolate bar's pretty good." Aeron waved it in Leah's face.

She swiped at him, barely missing her snack. "It has my name on it."

He flipped it around and examined it. "I don't see anything."

"Just because my handwriting is bad, does not mean I—" With her mouth open, her eyes narrowed, hyperfocusing on something or someone behind Aeron.

"Leah?" asked Cassian.

A man in a white lab coat raised from the middle of the stage with Felix and an older woman with a huge dress. The similarities between the man and Leah were uncanny. They had the same eyes, nose, and jaw structure.

Oh my gosh! I know him. Leah's neck and shoulders tensed, and her hand clenched into a fist.

"He's the one who came to tell us my dad had died," said Cassian.

Leah froze, refusing to face him.

Aeron munched on Leah's chocolate bar. "You know him too? He would visit with my dad a lot when I was a kid."

Felix sauntered to the front of the stage, causing the crowd to go wild. He held a microphone in his hand, and lights focused on him as if it was a stage production or talk show. "Ladies and Gentlemen, welcome to the 33rd Neforian Trials. I am one of your Trial Masters."

Chapter 10

Felix's talking seemed to drag on for eternity. Introductions and welcomes went in one ear and out the other. When would the action begin? Despite Felix's best effort and extreme charisma, he was not entertaining to Aeron in the least bit. He came for a good time and some adrenaline rushes, not boring speeches. A bit of residual frustration settled in his chest as he rested lazily on Leah's head. Cassian snorted while Leah tried pushing him aside.

"I am trying to pay attention," she said. She glared up at him, or tried to at least. His head pinned hers in place. "Get off."

"But you're exactly the right height." Aeron smiled. For some that acted emotionless, Leah got angry easily.

Focusing his attention back to Felix, he fought the boredom. Cassian shifted his weight, rocking back and forth impatiently on his heels. People were ducking around both Cassian and him because they blocked the view of the stage. They stood directly in the middle, almost under Felix.

"Pass her over," Cassian said, reaching for Leah.

Aeron wrapped his arms around her. "This is my head rest."

Leah tensed like a rock, and her breathing sped up. Her knife slipped into her hand. He quickly let go. "Sorry. It feels like I've known you forever, so I kinda forgot. I won't do it again." Aeron backed off.

She relaxed slightly. "All—all is forgiven."

"And now ladies and gentlemen, I would like to introduce you to our other Trial Masters. First, we have world renowned scientist, Alejandro Perez. With his world altering technology and the gull to make breakthroughs in science using illegal methods, he has come up with our third challenge. Frightening, isn't it?" Felix gave Alejandro a pointed look. "With the elegance and grace to rule over her own fiefdom despite the seemingly impossible barriers of the Neforian nation of Kazo, let me introduce you to Lady Elizabeth. Not only is she smart and powerful, but she is in charge of the first Trial, which will be explained shortly. The second Trial is run by yours truly, and I must go over it before the first Trial can even begin."

Elderly Lady Elizabeth performed a practiced curtsey in a dress that had as many layers as an onion. On the top of her head sat a white wig shaped as a bee's nest. Aeron thought he had seen her picture in one of the many history books he'd been forced to read as a child. He liked the woman immediately with her sharp gaze and wrinkles.

Felix smiled fondly at the old woman before opening his big mouth. His appearance flickered, revealing his true self. *How did he get a holographic disguise? Those cost an arm and a leg, and sometimes a kidney as well. Those are so convenient.* An admiration for Felix blossomed in Aeron. *I need to be friends with this guy.* Sadly, he didn't get to see what Felix looked like underneath the disguise.

"Get on with it, pretty boy," an elderly man, with stormy grey eyes and hair as white as Aeron's, shouted. Winking at Aeron, the man started booing.

"If you make any noise, Sheep brain, I will make sure you never speak again," Leah warned.

Aeron protested. "I wasn't going to do anything. I'm far above those petty things." He flipped his hair dramatically. *Sheep brain? Was she calling him dumb?* By the way Cassian laughed, he assumed yes. An unfamiliar feeling warmed his chest, and reddened his face.

"You alright? Your face is quite red." Cassian invaded Aeron's personal space, inspecting Aeron. Aeron tried to dodge, but Cassian slapped a cold hand on his forehead. "Well, it isn't a fever."

"I'm sorry to say this, but because of the influx of increasingly dangerous creatures, we have had to make the Trials even harder and deadlier than before. As you know, we made you sign a contract which signed away your family's rights to take legal action so we hope you are aware of the dangers you will face. On another note, the adventurer guilds are looking forward to having more exceptional people in their pockets." Aeron yawned.

"The first and third Trials have little instruction needed, but the second one has a few rules and guidelines. Your task is to make it to our Lirith garden within a week. Sounds easy, right? The caveat is that you'll be thrown into random areas of a small island made up of parts of the abyss. If you don't make it to the designated place within the seven days, you will be booted off the island and returned to this room. Those who pass will be taken to the third Trial."

Felix paused, looking around the room with solemn eyes. "Now Trial Runners, are you ready to begin?"

Aeron joined the outburst of cheers. This was it. His life would be so much better once the Trials started. *No clan pressure. No boring politicians. No more Mother. This is what I've been waiting for.* Cassian quivered next to him, and Leah covered her ears to block out the cheering and hollering.

With a piercing gaze, Lady Elizabeth examined Aeron and frowned. She gave Felix a polite nod before descending the stage. The crowd parted around her as she walked into the middle of the room. Blue lights flashed from her palms, creating large tubes of light that opened and closed like elevator doors.

"You must enter one of these portals in order to get to your destination. Fail to do so before the time is up, and you will be forced to leave. One must be careful or you perhaps will face terrible injury." Lady Elizabeth curtsied and exited the room.

Felix flashed a smile. "Good luck." He left the room through the hole in the stage floor.

Chaos broke out, the kind that sent most people into their deaths. People surged towards the portals as they opened and closed. Some disappeared completely once they shut. Multiple people could fit into one portal if timed properly. An arm rolled next to Aeron's foot from an unsuccessful attempt to cram people into the tube.

Adrenaline flooded into Aeron's system as the bloodshed worsened. The less competitors, the easier the Trials would be. Some Trial Runners bit each other like wild animals. Pushing and pulling ended up in lost limbs and heads. Screaming and yelling resounded on the metal walls, and blood pooled and spread on the stainless steel.

A few of the animal-like Trial Runners raced towards them. *Understandably. Three young people standing in a group are going to draw attention. Too bad for them. I am much more capable than most of these people combined.*

One woman with teeth like a shark lunged at him while Cassian fended himself from her partner, a large man with the same shark teeth. They were a joke. They had no technique, no strength. Just an average pair of below average people. He laughed, taking out the woman with a knife to her throat.

Cassian blocked all of the man's punches with great ease, but never countered with his own. *What is he doing? He could easily get rid of him.* Cassian crouched down, blocking a hard swing that made the guy unbalanced. Leah used Cassian as a springboard, wrapped her legs around the man's bulging neck, and used her legs to choke him out. Cassian moved out of the way. As he came down, Leah untangled her legs. She fell into a roll, popping up as quickly as she could. Her hair fell into her eyes, and she fought to get it out.

Aeron nodded in approval, a little disappointed that she didn't finish the job, but he could fix that. A blue light flashed next to him. Without comprehending what was happening, he pushed Cassian and Leah into the portal.

It was a tight squeeze. Leah was sandwiched in between Cassian and him. Her eyebrows furrowed.

"Is being sandwiched comfortable?" asked Aeron.

Leah had no time to answer as light flooded his vision, and they shot up into the air. The contents of his stomach rose into his mouth. Leah swore under her breath before gagging. Aeron felt bad for vomiting on her.

Chapter 11

Sunlight flooded her eyes as the tube-like portal opened up. Vomit flew everywhere as the blue light fizzled away, but the scent lingered on her hair and clothes. They weren't even an hour into the Trials, but she already needed to shower desperately. Throwing up didn't make Leah feel any better. Her stomach rumbled, and she felt the urge to hurl once again. Swallowing the upcoming vomit, she took in her surroundings. Her body ached from trying to be in the portal without touching the others.

Aeron and Cassian kneeled next to her heaving out whatever was left of their meals. Cassian rolled onto his back, trying to catch his breath. The contents of his backpack poured out on the grass. Aeron placed his hands on the ground. He attempted to stand, but went back onto his knees.

"Never again," Aeron said before throwing up again.

Grass tickled her ankles and not in a pleasant way. Whoever said grass was soft was a liar, and Leah would find them and rub their face in this grass. Maybe being stabbed by the prickly blades would wake them up to reality. Leah drew in her irritation, fear, and confusion. She folded the emotions neatly in her box.

Trees encompassed the area. Green leaves rustled on their branches. Instead of being a dark and dangerous forest around her, sun filtered in between the tall and dark trunks , illuminating more plant life. Pink, white, and yellow flowers caught the wind, bringing her the fresh scent of spring and allergies. She sneezed, and her stomach lurched.

Birds sang their morning songs as a reiderak dipped its snout into the little babbling brook which was at the heart of the meadow. Aeron rolled down a little hill. He crouched and crawled over towards the rare creature. Instead of the usual predatory look he donned, child-like curiosity sparkled in his eyes.

Like most individuals, Leah never in her twenty years laid her eyes on a reiderak. She couldn't look away even if she wanted to. Her focus was glued onto the creature. They lived a very long time and only had a few offspring every decade. Leah felt sympathy for the creature, sought by many because there were only a few. *What a sad and difficult life to live.* She shook her head and put on a face of indifference.

It ruffled its ombre feathers, starting at the top with a sky blue trailing to a shadow's gray. The beast stalked over to her with strong powerful legs that could carry it for miles. She gulped as she noticed the sharp teeth that hung out of its jowls and determined diamond eyes, clearer than the sky. Its body was like a deer, long and lean, but the reiderak was not prey, but a predator. It was the king of the skies, with an ivory crown of antlers entwined on its head.

She froze in her spot. The reiderak looked into her eyes. Bumping their noses together, it ran off, losing three feathers. With a woosh, giant wings unfurled and it leapt into the air. It flew around her head before taking off into the skies and vanished from sight. Leah's heart beat like hummingbird wings. Hesitantly, she picked up the feathers. They were soft and warm like a freshly dried blanket.

Leah dunked her head into the brook, washing as much of the vomit out of her hair and off her clothes. *He could've at least tried to avoid me,* she grumbled under her breath as she attempted to make herself smell better.

"I never imagined seeing a reiderak." Cassian's eyes were bright with excitement. He stuffed the feathers into his backpack along with the rest of the contents that had fallen out.

Leah walked toward the edge of the meadow. If she didn't say anything, they wouldn't notice her absence. The two of them made her feel as if she was suffocating. How they had so much energy was beyond her. She couldn't be involved with them much longer. A beam of red light forming in the sky caught her attention. *Is that where the garden is?*

As she passed the tree line, she noticed Aeron walking by her side. His footsteps fell silently into the thick underbrush. A thin trail had been forged from years of animals walking on through it. A bird squawked and landed on a nearby tree, scouting out the area for small prey. Leah randomly turned to escape from the dumb boy and bumped her nose into Cassian's sternum. She bit her lip to keep her words inside.

After taking three more steps, Leah whipped around to face them. "What do you two think you are doing?"

"Sticking together?" Cassian answered, obviously confused.

"No." She had to put her foot down there. Aeron snorted, releasing more of her ire. "This is not a team effort. I do not need you. You will be a—a burden."

"Why are you here, Leah?" Cassian asked, as if the question would help convince her that he wasn't going to be a waste of time and energy. Time and energy she didn't have.

Leah looked directly in his face. Her eyes narrowed and she crossed her arms. "I could ask you the same thing. What about the most suspicious person here, Aeron?"

Cassian shifted on a pile of fallen leaves. Their crunch startled him. He laughed sheepishly and moved away from the pile.

"I'm in no way suspicious. Look at this face." Aeron pointed at himself and gave a confident smile. Leah rolled her eyes. "But since you want me to go first, I will oblige. I was bored."

"No! I would've never guessed," Cassian said sarcastically which made Aeron laugh. "I want to discover more of the abyss. Only the top three sectors are occupied by immigrants ,and no one's returned from the sixth sector. I want to be the first to explore the whole abyss, and find the legendary city of Katharnia."

"Katharnia's just a myth," Aeron said, eyeing a red fox as it snuck by.

Cassian glared at him. "There's evidence."

"Fake evidence. It can't be real."

"I thought you liked fun and adventure." Cassian pouted. "Plus, we've got artifacts and historical documents that show its existence."

"Sheep brain lives for blood and guts, not true fun," Leah said. "He probably cannot read those documents you are talking about."

"That's so mean." Cassian said, and Aeron laughed. Cassian looked around briefly as if making sure no one could hear what he was about to say. "But it's not my only reason for going. I've never told anyone this, but I think something happened to my dad. I mean, he's dead and has been for a long time. It's just some stuff isn't adding up." He looked away. "I just want to see if what I was told and what happened actually align, you know?"

Leah choked a bit. They didn't seem to notice her moment of panic. *How would he know?*

"You don't give me the revenge guy vibes." Aeron leaned against the tree, and while he was focused on Leah, she knew he was keeping a steady watch around them. "You haven't told us your reason yet. You can't wimp out."

"I made a promise," she said. With all the self-discipline she had, which wasn't a lot, she forced indifference in her voice. Her heart felt like it was breaking as she thought on it.

Cassian sighed. "What was the promise?"

"I promised my companions that I would save them. They just happen to be in the abyss. Why do I even have to tell you? It is never going to be your business." Leah grumbled. "Nosey people meet quick ends."

"Interesting." Large poisonous ants crawled onto Aeron's shoulder which he brushed off as if they were regular insects. "So what you are saying is that you're afraid of having emotional attachment because you have no friends?"

Cassian's eyes went wide and he shook his head in warning. Looking at Leah, he sighed.

Leah got up into Aeron's face or tried to. Her short stature prevented her from being aggressive in his space. He stared down at her and Leah's cool crumbled.

"I fear nothing," she growled.

"Nothing but human attachment," he countered. His eyes were bright with laughter. He had no guard up.

The wind rustled the trees and birds chirped. None of them moved. Tension sparked between Leah and Aeron. She tore at her lip with her teeth, and then she calmed. All emotions rearranged in her box. Aeron's excitement died with the lack of reaction from her.

She backed out of his space and walked away. Cassian grabbed her sweater sleeve. With a glance over her shoulder, she shrugged him off. He had a look of fear and disappointment. Alayna made that face a lot.

"Leah, please, let's do this together." His voice trembled. "Can't you make an exception to whatever you're going through? I want to survive this with you."

Her heart wavered. Stupid, stupid emotions. Always getting the best of her when she needed distance. She stood very still. A war of emotions played in her inside. She felt so confused and nauseous. Swallowing both down, she let out an exasperated sigh.

Dealing with people got to her. It always did. That's why she was so attached to Felix. He was everything that she was not. He could bear his emotions. Leah could barely handle her shadow. Cassian knew how to manipulate her. Aeron hit the nail right on the head.

She was afraid. Afraid of what could happen to those around her. Afraid of what they would do to her. Leah knew another betrayal would lead to her demise.

"Please, Leah. I know I won't get in your way." Cassian batted his eyes innocently.

"No."

"Come on. What harm will it do?"

"She's a chicken." Aeron moved away from the tree and headed up the road. "Her fear is controlling her."

Cassian grabbed her hands. "It's okay to be scared. This will help you overcome your fears."

I am going to kill this Sefic boy. Leah clenched her jaw; her teeth ground together.

"I want collateral." Leah compromised her emotions and Cassian's begging. She just needed to find her treasure. She could last for a while with them as long as they risked as much as she would.

Aeron ran his hand through his hair. "How about our lives?"

"Absolutely not." Cassian's mouth dropped. "Aeron, I think you need therapy. Why would you use your life as collateral?"

"The one who needs therapy isn't me, but using our life is quite common." Aeron smiled. "Do you know what an assassin's blood bonds are?"

Cassian shook his head. Leah had never heard of it either, and she had personally met many of the Sefic offspring.

"It links the flow of life between people. They become closer than blood families because some sort of magic binds them to certain conditions. Betrayal being one of them. We never use it in a positive setting. We tend to bind our clients to us so that they can't spill their guts. The punishment of betrayal is a painful gruesome death, caused by whatever magic binds the two individuals." Aeron's seriousness startled Leah.

Cassian tapped his chin. "I don't like it, but I would never betray you guys."

Aeron threw his arm around Cassian's shoulder. "I can't imagine you have a deceivous bone in your body."

"It sounds promising," Leah said after contemplating it. "I shall participate."

Aeron motioned for them to sit. Sticks poked into her legs, but she did not complain. The wind felt nice. Cassian pulled out a cup for Aeron while Aeron found a small dagger.

"Slice your finger with this knife and let the blood drip into the cup," he explained. "I'll go first."

Without hesitation, he opened up the skin of his finger. Crimson blood dribbled down his fingertip into the cup. He wiped it off and passed the knife to Cassian, who was distracted grabbing bandaids. He hurriedly handed one off to Aeron. Aeron stared at it for a moment before opening it up and sticking the fire truck bandaid on his finger.

"This seems sort of unsanitary," Cassian mumbled as he let his finger bleed into the cup.

Next, it was Leah's turn. She sighed. "It will take a second for me."

"How come?" Aeron cocked his head like a puppy does.

She sliced open her wrist. Both Cassian and Aeron yelped in shock. The skin pieced itself together before any blood left the wound. It itched as it closed up. Cassian looked so sad. *Why does he always look at me like that? It's natural.*

Aeron grabbed her wrist and felt where the wound had been. His eyes grew as round as saucers. He thumbed her wrist until he realized how weird it was. "Magic?" Aeron questioned.

Leah contemplated for a second. "Genetics."

"What people have these genetics?"

"Do not ask questions you are not prepared to hear the answer to," Leah said with finality. "Pain still occurs. I can prevent the wound from closing by keeping the weapon in the skin or by putting it in liquid." Leah sliced open her finger and kept the knife in her skin. Her breath hitched, but she let it out slowly when enough blood had formed outside of the wound. "There. We can now complete the binding."

Cassian grimaced as he always did when her body healed instantly. A sadness lingered on his face before he flashed her a smile, knowing he won this argument. Leah rolled her eyes and pushed her hair away from her face.

"Interesting. The longer I'm around you, the more mysterious you get. It's like a fun puzzle which is rare because puzzles are boring," said Aeron cheerfully. With an amused glance, he swiped their mixed blood onto Cassian's wrist. Cassian repeated it on her. Leah finalized the circle.

"Now, grab the wrist of the person you marked. It should basically make a triangle." Aeron's arm was warm between Leah's fingers. "I'll say the binding words, since I doubt you two have any inkling of the assassin's cant. Holva eleska mortum," Aeron whispered.

The blood line on their wrists glowed a strange red before fading into their skin. It seared hot against her flesh. The pounding of her heart only made the pain worse. Memories flashed in her mind. *Bodies, so many bodies.*

It stopped, the searing and the memories. Cassian was too enamored with their new bond to notice her brief panic, examining his wrist and feeling where the blood used to be, but Aeron's gaze burned holes in the side of her head.

Chapter 12

The portal appeared directly over Sebastian who narrowly ducked out of the way. Silas strutted into the blue beam with two women he had befriended early by his side. Silas smiled and flirted with them as the portal slowly closed, giving some more attendees hope. One of the ladies scoffed at Silas. She was laughing at the angry crease of his brow. In his hurt pride, he pushed her out of the portal as it closed. Getting caught partly in the tube, half of her body collapsed outside of the beam.

Sebastian's heart beat uncomfortably as he ran to her, but she had died immediately. *Silas killed someone. He—he just ended a woman's life for no reason.* Blood pooled underneath her. With trembling fingers, he closed her eye to bring him some peace in the situation. *How could Silas do this?* Tears threatened to spill out.

Silas abandoned him again. Sebastian was finally free, but a great loneliness suffocated him. He shouldn't feel conflicted, but Silas genuinely cared for Sebastian. He just didn't know how to show it properly. Sebastian rubbed his bruised ribs. He wore leather gloves in order to hide the swelling in his hand.

He looked around frantically. Fewer and fewer portals opened up, but more and more corpses piled on the floor. Severed limbs scattered far from their bodies. It was a battlefield. Sebastian stood and wandered around like a lost sheep. He checked on some of the contestants, trying to save at least one of the dying and spare them from this ongoing suffering.

The first trial was coming to a close. There was only one open portal, and Sebastain was the only one standing of the contestants. Despite his fellow Trial Masters' departure, Alejandro Perez watched from his spot on the stage

The Trial Master and scientist dropped off the stage and walked over to him. His white lab coat was stained red at the bottom. Sebastian stepped out of the way for the man. The crazy look in his eyes struck fear into Sebastian's already emotional heart. He stumbled on a loose arm. Using the momentum from Sebastian's fall, the man pushed him into the last portal. Sebastian almost lost his foot when he tumbled into the beam.

For the first time in his life, Sebastian experienced motion sickness in the portal. He believed it was a combination of watching so many people die and being abandoned that contributed to his queasiness. The images scarred his mind. His traumatic incident added them to its collection in his brain. Not too long ago, the most traumatic event was when Silas cut their faces. Now, his memories—his life—held very little more than trauma.

He tumbled out of the portal and landed in hot sand. Sebastian vomited, and the sun beat down on his dark skin. It was blazing hot. He forced himself onto shaky legs. Sebastian took three deep breaths and investigated the area. His eyes wandered across golden sand and dunes.

He'd been dropped off in the desert. Luckly, an oasis was nearby, and he could reside there until these stupid trials were over. Sebastian couldn't fight. *Why did that Trial Master force me into this? I had finally gotten free.*

Pondering over the illegal intervention, Sebastian trotted over to the oasis. Sweat dripped down his arms and legs. His shoulders sagged in relief as he neared the palm tree lined sanctuary. A colorful bird sat on the top of one singing a pretty tune. There was a clear pool of water and lush green vegetation. A red beam of light shot into the sky behind the oasis, far past the desert. *That's where Silas is headed to. It would be too tempting for him to not follow the obvious signs. As long as I don't go there, I'll be free.* He swallowed a lump in his throat.

Upon entering what he thought would be his safe haven, Sebastian lost all faith in humanity. His brother stood shirtless by the pond's shore. The woman who was in the portal with Silas stood beside him. She gave his brother a look that made Sebastian shiver uncomfortably. Silas had a mysterious way with women that Sebastian couldn't understand. He hesitated, not wanting to step foot where Silas was, but also wanting to see if his brother was uninjured.

In his moment of hesitation, Silas caught sight of Sebastian. He walked over and hugged Sebastian. It was so comforting that Sebastian sagged a bit. All thoughts of escaping Silas were gone. He was alright after all.

"I worried about ya," Silas said as he pulled away. He pointed to the woman next to him. She was tall and muscular. "This is ma new girlfrien'. What's yer name, Love?"

She licked her lips and batted her eyes. "Marina."

Sebastian's voice caught in his throat. This was why they were in the trials anyway. His inability to keep his hands off every living, breathing woman ruined Sebastian's life. Sebastian gaped at Silas, but straightened his expression when Silas looked his way.

"She'll be travelin' with us." Silas wrapped his arm around her waist and kissed her cheek. She giggled and curled into him. "I hope ya get along."

Sebastian wanted to cry.

Chapter 13

Cassian kept looking at his wrist despite the scar completely fading hours ago. He felt it still underneath his skin. It was a burning that ran from his wrist to his heart. He knew that no matter where Leah and Aeron went, he'd be able to find them. If anything happened to them, he would know. It twisted his heart to think that as soon as one of them died, the bond would tell him. At least that's what Aeron said, but Cassian wondered if he had only been teasing them. The three of them linked together for the rest of their lives, and Leah and Aeron didn't even like each other.

Leah and Aeron stood next to each other, facing the woods, and arguing. Leah's arms were crossed as Aeron towered over her. Leah refused to back down. A fire of disdain burned in her eyes.

"If we go through the woods here, it will take us closer to the beam," Leah explained for what seemed like the millionth time.

Aeron rolled his eyes. "That's what you think. We have no idea what's on either side, so why can't we check out the far side of the woods? You just want to be in control, but let's be real, you've got no idea what's going on."

"It is not like you know what is happening either."

"At least I'm not pretending like you are."

"At least I'm not pretending like you are," she mocked. "When do you not pretend? You are a Sefic."

Aeron glared at her. "Just because I'm a Sefic?"

"You would know better than I."

Cassian walked over to them, stepping between them. He took a breath, channeling his inner Amyra. "Will you two quit it? The sun is starting to set, and we've made no progress. Did you two forget that we only have seven days to find this garden?"

Aeron looked away from Cassian. *My expression is nowhere as scary as Mom's. He's overreacting.* Leah kicked at the ground, refusing to make eye contact. *Maybe I'm just really good at this.*

"Apologies." She glared at Aeron from the corner of her eye.

"I for one, am not sorry." Aeron laughed at the shock that slipped across Cassian's face. "I'm kidding, but will finish this conversation later, Shrimp."

"Sure we will."

Cassian shook his head, ignoring the obvious disgust Aeron and Leah held for each other. A cool breeze blew across Cassian's face, and bile rose in his throat. *The sea.* He smelled the sea. The deep body of water that tore apart all those who succumbed to it was in walking distance. It made him sick. In contrast to him, both Leah and Aeron perked up. It was the brightest Leah's eyes ever shined, and her guard loosened up ever so slightly.

Chattering sounded from the meadow. Someone let out a bark-like laugh. Cassian crept towards the treeline. Leah crouched and crawled into the shadows of a tree. Her body blending into the tree and under-brush as she made her way further into the woods. Cassian caught sight of her hair when she slipped behind a tree. Aeron swiftly ran into the woods and climbed into the thick branches of a large tree. A few leaves fell as Aeron tried to get comfortable within the foliage. Cassian flattened himself into the ground and crawled into a bush. Thorns cut into his skin, and for a terrifying moment, his backpack got stuck. He yanked it hard, tearing it a little, but successfully pulled it into the bush.

"I hope I find that arrogant cad and his disgusting little friends soon," a slithery voice said right in front of Cassian. The man kicked a rock into the bush, and it bounced off Cassian's cheek.

More feet joined up with the slithery man. They stomped around like newborn dragons, creating a loud ruckus as they kicked trees and bushes. The men wandered into the woods, but never walked close to Leah or Aeron.

"Your brother has friends?" A feminine voice replied way too quickly.

Another man let out a harsh laugh. "The great and mighty Aeron Sefic, renowned all over the assassin's world as the next head of the clans, has friends? Now, that's hilarious."

After searching around for a few minutes, the other group grew discouraged and walked out of the woods.

"I could've sworn I saw them over here," said the woman as she made her way into the meadow.

As soon as they were out of sight, Cassian crawled out of his bush. His muscles were cramping, and a few cuts on his arms bled. Aeron fell out of his tree, landed on his back awkwardly, and weezed. Leah emerged from the shadows and stood over Aeron.

"Ow," Aeron managed to say through gasps of air. "That's pretty embarrassing."

"Are you alright?" Cassian asked as he jogged over.

Aeron sat up, rubbed the back of his neck, and glared at Leah whose lips were pressed flat against her face as she fought a laugh. "I'm just fine. Go on. I know you want to laugh, shrimp."

Shaking her head, Leah held her laughter in.

I wish she trusted us more.

"Was that not your brother?" asked Leah.

"It was, but I'm not sure who else was with him." Aeron smiled. "He's an idiot to think *we're* friends, but even more so to think I'd die in a week-long game."

A breeze brought back the overwhelming smell of salt water and sand, and Cassian gagged. He hated the ocean. The dancing waves and immense depth drove him mad. It definitely didn't help that he was told his father had died in the fourth sector which was known for having a large ocean. "What now?"

"Let us follow the ocean breeze," Leah said. Her body pointed to the direction of the salty water.

"Sounds good to me." Aeron with the help of Cassian stood. He rubbed his lower back like an elderly man. "Man, that hurt way worse than I originally thought. I should've found a sturdier branch."

Cassian nodded, but his hands clenched so tight that his nails left imprints on his palm. He couldn't let them down, so he kept his mouth shut and tried to take deep breaths through his nose. Sweat dripped down the back of his shirt. It was only water. There was no need for him to get in it.

It took mere moments to reach the shoreline and Cassian held his breath. His heart settled at the top of his throat, and he just couldn't quite get it to go all the way back where it was supposed to be. Each beat of his heart brought more nerves to the surface.

He admitted that the sight brought a little admiration for nature. The sand glistened like gold from the afternoon sun. Cassian hadn't realized how much time had passed. Waves gently rolled back and forth. Clouds and birds reflected on its clear surface, but he saw strange shadows under the beauty. He gulped.

Standing with her feet in the water, Leah looked at peace. Her eyes closed as she bathed in the sunlight. The wind caught up her pink hair and brushed it softly behind her. With the sun hitting her skin, it looked as if she had been spun from caramel. With large cliffs surrounding the outlet, a portrait of her fairy-esque features was painted into Cassian's memories.

Aeron openly gawked, leaving Cassian with a mixture of pride and irritation. He appreciated Aeron's eye for beauty, but Leah was pretty much Cassian's sister. They weren't blood related, but Leah had made his dream come true. He had asked for a sister for at least three birthdays, but all his dad would do was laugh and tell him maybe. From the time he could talk, Cassian had wanted a sister.

"I used to live by the ocean when I was small," Leah said quietly. Cassian barely heard it over the waves that ebbed and flowed onto the shoreline.

Aeron took his shoes off and padded over to the water. He immediately jumped out. "It's so cold. Why do you look so lonely?"

"I do not look lonely."

He scoffed. "Don't lie. My youngest sibling makes that look whenever I tell her I have to leave."

Cassian tried to get a glimpse of her expression, but he was too far away to see it. He did see the dark shadow that slithered through the water. "Leah!"

It was too late. A tentacle wrapped around her leg and dragged her beneath the water. Aeron reached for her, stepping into the water. He was flung up in the air by another tentacle. The tentacle caught him by the leg and dangled him upside down.

"Aeron!" Cassian screamed. He got as close to the shoreline as he could.

His heart hammered in his chest as the creature brought Leah out of the water. Both Aeron and Leah swung at their tentacles with tiny daggers, but despite their best efforts, the creature took no damage.

"Do something! You are an assassin." Leah yelled.

"Assassins usually do things stealthily, and there's nothing stealthy about this situation. You do something. You seem like you have something mysterious going on so you might have something useful." He let himself dangle in the air as if he couldn't bother fighting for his life.

Leah continued to slash at her tentacle furiously. "If I had something like that, I would have used it already!"

All fear left Cassian as the two of them fought. "Will you two stop bickering! Your lives are in danger."

"It's not like you're helping." Aeron crossed his arms.

"I'm trying. That thing is ridiculously large and I am afraid of large bodies of water. I'm trying my best." His throat felt raw from screaming.

Cassian moved into the water. He stood paralyzed as the water lapped at his ankles. *There's no time to be afraid, Cassian! Move. Think.*

Do something. A tingling sensation ran through his body. He forced his eyes up and away from the water. The tentacle dunked Aeron into the water, holding the assassin under the surface. Aeron struggled under the water. Cassian frantically reached for him, and a beam of water burst from the ocean, hitting the tentacle at such speeds that it left a large cut in its flesh. The tentacle loosened around Aeron, giving him enough room to escape.

Aeron swam as fast as he could. He pulled up onto the shore, out of breath and swearing. He crawled away from the water's edge and rolled over as soon as he thought he was safe. "It was—it was a huge freaking kraken."

What just happened? Cassian's hands shook, and a random wave of exhaustion hit him hard. *This can wait. Leah is still in dange—*

The kraken's mouth and all of its thousands of teeth raised out of the water. Leah swayed precariously over its mouth. She stopped fighting it. Her arms hung limply over her head.

"Aeron, what do I do?" asked Cassian. His voice shook.

Aeron coughed. "Use your transcendence."

"My what?"

"Transcendence. You know? The thing you did for me. Just wave your arms or something." Aeron sat up.

Whilst he was seeking counsel, the kraken dropped Leah. She dove straight into the kraken. He shut his eyes tightly and slashed both of his arms down, praying something would happen. There was a large splash and an ear shattering shriek, but Cassian was too afraid to look.

"Are you going to go—" Aeron started. "Never mind. I'll do it."

Cassian's head pounded and limbs shook. He fell to his knees, splashing cool water on his overheating face. In the distance, he heard patterned splashing, but he couldn't seem to open his eyes.

Leah sunk down into the depths of the water. Her lungs screamed for oxygen, but she was too tired to fight the ocean. *She will forgive me, right? I tried my best, so she cannot blame me. I was just another casualty.* Her eyes stung from the salt water. She closed them and let herself continue to drown. Her body couldn't hold on, and she breathed in water. It burned even worse than before as if fire was being swallowed, not water.

I made a promise, but I failed to keep it again. I was not even worth saving. This is for the best. Something wrapped around her waist, dragging her up to the surface. Air brushed against her face, but she still couldn't breathe. *I am sorry, Alayna...*

Chapter 14

Why did I agree to follow them?

Sebastian reluctantly walked behind Silas and Marina as they led the way through a sandy beach, contemplating his life choices. *I should've just ran when I saw him. Why do I keep going back?* His heart twisted with guilt. Silas needed him. He wouldn't survive long without Sebastian helping him. At least that was what Sebastian told himself over and over again.

Sunlight began to fade into dusk, but the beam of red light brightened up the sky. It seemed just as far away as it had been hours before when they were walking through the desert. Sebastian hoped and prayed that they wouldn't run into anyone else on this terrible journey. *If I fail this test, I can just go home, but how am I going to tell Silas?*

With aching feet and pain in his rib, Sebastian's desire for rest grew. He stopped and leaned against a tree. The bark scraped his skin through his shirt.

Marina turned back and watched him intensely. A smile lit up her face, but it wasn't meant for him. Her eyes crinkled up. She faced forward and dragged Silas away from Sebastian. Sebastian's heart quickened as he pushed himself off the tree. *Why is she taking Silas away?* She shooed at Sebastian. Silas let out an odd laugh, but ignored Sebastian as he had this whole trip. He sighed and trudged behind them.

The setting sun flooded Sebastian's eyes, and the sea reflected the light, illuminating the shoreline. Reds, oranges, and blues painted the sky and sea. Something floated just off the shore, but Sebastian couldn't quite tell what it was. Looking around him, he snuck away from Silas and Marina to get a better look.

As he walked through the sand, a man emerged out of the water, pulling a body with him. His arms shook as he dragged the body away from the sea's greeting reach. Sebastian ran to the man as he began chest compressions. He barrelled up to the man whose hair was white as snow. Sebastian almost didn't notice another man with brown hair and tanned skin lying half way in the water. He forced himself to take a deep breath. *The sea hasn't taken him yet so he'll be alright for now.*

"You're doing a great job," Sebastian encouraged, kneeling on the other side of the woman. "Marina! Get the man out of the water."

"Got it," Marina answered and ran across the sand.

The man stiffened, but continued to do chest compressions. His brows were furrowed in concentration. "Come on, Shrimp. You've got to pull through this. I haven't solved your mystery yet."

Concern ran through Sebastian as he checked the woman's pulse. He felt nothing at all. Her skin was cold and wet from the water. *It may be too late. Oh Lord, I hope not.*

"Try giving her mouth to mouth," Sebastian instructed. He kept his face calm and friendly to help keep the man from panicking. "Only two breaths though. You need to make sure her heart starts."

The man pinched the woman's nose, and Silas helped hold her head in place to keep her airway open. The man forced as much air into her lungs and continued chest compressions. Nothing. Time was running out.

Silas stood behind the man, casting a shadow over the woman's lifeless body. "Don't tell ma girlfrien' what to do," Silas said.

"Shut up, Silas. Also, would you back off? Your presence isn't helpful." Sebastian felt a weak pulse, and hope overwhelmed him. *She might make it!* "You can stop chest compressions."

The woman coughed and coughed. She rolled over, and water cleared out of her lungs. She was barely awake, gasping as much oxygen as she could. His eyes were filled with confusion.

Silas moved closer. "Yer disrespect is unacceptable."

The man whipped around with a dagger in his hand. Sebastian never saw him pull it out. Silas stopped immediately.

"Come any closer, and I'll kill the both of you. Got it?" His arms held strong despite the obvious exhaustion in his voice. "I'm too tired right now to deal with any inconveniences."

"Aeron, it's okay," the other man said. He dragged his feet as he collapsed next to the woman. He grabbed her hand tenderly. Her chest rose and fell in even motions. "Thank God, she's alive."

Marina walked up to Silas and grabbed his hand. She attempted to calm his seething but earned a slap in the face instead. The two men, Aeron and his companion, jumped. Marina held her cheek in shock. Her face reddened, and she slapped Silas back. Sebastian, Aeron, and his companion scooted away.

Aeron's friend turned away from the heated argument going on behind them. "I'm Cassian. Thank you so much for helping Aeron save my sister." Cassian gave him a friendly smile.

"It was nothing." Sebastian waved off the thanks.

Aeron laughed. It was a deep and warm sound. "No really. This was my first time trying to save someone. I mean, I knew the basic concept from way back in my training days, but I've never had to use them."

The argument grew louder. Cassian peeked over his shoulder, and shrugged when he met Aeron's eyes. Sebastian wanted a close bond like that.

Sebastian cocked his head, noticing how dirty his glasses were as the last bit of sunlight exposed the streaks. "What do you mean?"

The woman shifted and groaned. "My ribs."

"Nice to see you're up, Leah." Aeron pushed his wet hair out of his face, slickening it straight back. "You've got no right to complain after I saved your life."

"I will complain. I am in pain," she said quietly before letting out a pained laugh.

She shouldn't be this aware after drowning. "I'm Sebastian by the way. The two arguing are my brother, Silas, and Marina, his new girl-friend. I know you don't know me, but I'm rather worried about your physical state. I mean, you just drowned after all. Would you mind if I do a quick check up?"

"I do mind," she answered, staring up at him.

Sebastian slumped. *I kind of figured, but I'm a bit worried. She seems pretty nervous though.* The yelling turned into screaming behind Cassian, but Sebastian ignored them.

"But as you helped this Elikar, I will give you a chance. Someone help me up." She wrapped an arm around Cassian's neck as he helped her sit. She grimaced in pain. "Everything hurts."

Sebastian pulled out the mini flashlight from his pocket. "Look straight ahead."

He shined the light in her eyes. *Pupils are normal. I don't see any-thing here. That's good.* "How does your head feel?"

"A little off, but that was probably from the lack of oxygen, or being dropped from the kraken," she said. "I would not be able to tell you."

A gunshot rang across the emptiness. Sebastian's three acquaint-ances shot up. Leah crumpled back to the ground, holding her ribs. Sebastian moved closer to her and helped her sit up normally. She bit her lip until it bled. He gasped as he watched the split heal itself.

"Do not look forward," she said to him. "I fear it will only pain you."

Sebastian wanted to listen to her. He meant to, but he glanced. Silas stood in the rising moon's light. A wicked grin spread across his face. With a crazed look, Silas narrowed in on Leah and Sebastian. Marina lay on the sand with a bullet through her brain. Blood spread across the sand. Sweat ran down Sebastian's back.

"Don't think I won't shoot ya too," said Silas, waving the gun around dangerously. "Yer gonna help get me to this garden, and I don't wanna hear a word from ya. Got it?"

Aeron took a step forward, and Silas trained the gun onto him. Sebastian clenched his jaw to keep it from chattering. Aeron kept his eyes focused on Silas, but Silas's gaze flickered to Leah and Sebastian, the weak links.

"We'll come with you without a fight," Cassian said quietly. "Please don't shoot."

Silas let his guard down as he smiled. Aeron whipped around, an argument ready to be fired, but his legs were shaking from what Sebastian assumed was exertion rather than fear. Cassian shook his head and pointed to Leah who was breathing raggedly. Her eyes were drooping, and her body swayed.

Aeron strutted over to Leah, helped her to her feet, and forced her to move away from Sebastian. Leah sighed, but the tension in her shoulders loosened up.

"Be nicer to her. She just came back from the dead," said Cassian. "Don't ignore me because you think you can take them on."

Sebastian quivered. He stood to join Silas, looking back at their three prisoners. *How many more people will Silas drag to hell with him?*

Chapter 15

Cassian hated to admit that he was panicking. Again. His back leaned against a cold boulder, protecting most of him from the cold night's breeze. The backpack he had brought was being held and ransacked by Silas. Leah and Aeron had almost died, and both were too weak from the encounter with the kraken to fight, not that Cassian was doing much better compared to them.

Stars twinkled above him, and the moon covered the sand in its silver light. There was a slight breeze. The ocean filled the silence with its rhythmic waves. What should've been a beautiful and comforting scene terrified him. Turning his head too far, he saw the woman's body. Cassian's stomach did an uncomfortable twist as he tried to force the sight from his mind.

Across from the little fire in front of him was their captor. Silas poked at the fire as Sebastian prepared a meal. The smell of burning fish flooded Cassian's nostrils. Sebastian had seemed just fine too. *How could I be so stupid? I should've been more aware.*

Leah's head settled against Cassian's arm. She breathed softly as she slept against his arm. Her clothes were still damp, and she shivered.

The day caught up with all of them. His body ached, and each movement brought sudden pain. A headache formed at the back of his neck, but in the midst of his body's suffering, a new feeling flowed through his body—powerful and calming like the ocean waves that rolled in and out in the silvery moonlight. It pulsed with his heartbeat. It was comforting like a hug from his dad, warm and familiar.

Aeron sat on the other side of Leah. He huddled close to her, trying to warm himself up with the fire and the little body heat she had. His hair had dried slicked back, and the salt water made it stick in place. A small scar faded from time cut into his forehead from his hairline.

"What do you want?" asked Aeron. He refused to look directly at Cassian.

"You're finally talking to me." Cassian smiled. "I thought two hours was a pretty long time to pettily ignore someone."

Aeron scoffed. "I could've taken him out easily."

"Dude, you were shaking like a leaf. There was no way. He'd have shot all of us dead." Cassian shifted so Leah's head wouldn't scoot further down his arm.

"Yeah, but dead is better than captured." Aeron glared at the twins. "And I wasn't shaking like a leaf."

"You totally were."

Sebastian stood up and walked over to them with a fire roasted fish for each of them and himself. He handed one to Cassian who took it gratefully. Aeron eyed him the whole time as he snatched his away from Sebastian.

"Leah probably won't eat that," said Cassian with a mouthful of hot fish in his mouth.

"But she needs to eat." Concern filled Sebastian's voice. "Though I particularly would not want to eat fish either. So would one of you like mine?"

As Aeron took the other fish, Cassian nudged Leah awake. She woke up speaking, panicked Lirithian, and grabbed Cassian's arm. Her fingers dug into his skin, and her voice grew more panicked. She looked around in the dark night, meeting Sebastian's startled eyes. Leah was still half asleep.

"I don't know what you're saying," Sebastian said. He took a step away from her.

"You're alright, Leah." Cassian grabbed her in an attempt to keep her still. Worry creased his brow. His touch seemed to wake her fully, but she was shaking. She covered her ears with her hands.

She faced Aeron. "Aeine lumino deca? Surano telisumase marenon."

"Elio. Methani hufo." Aeron answered in Lirithian. His brows were furrowed. "Lumino dera zuo elerso momiya yeruse."

Leah relaxed, settled back against the rock, and uncovered her ears. Cassian released her, and she rubbed her arms. "Apologies. I was a bit confused. You are offering food, yes?"

Sebastian nodded and walked closer to her. He cautiously handed her the fish. "Are you alright?"

Leah immediately handed the fish to Cassian. "I am doing just fine. Though I believe this may be my first meal of the day."

Knowing the drill, Cassian took a bite of the fish. "So that's why you took it," he said with food in his mouth.

Leah watched intensely as Cassian chewed and swallowed. Her stares made him a little uncomfortable, but she was making sure nothing was in the food. Aeron raised his brows when Leah started eating the fish quietly. Recognition glimmered in Sebastian's eyes.

"Sebastian! What are ya still doin' over there?" said Silas. "Yer not supposed to hang around our prisoners."

Sebastian cringed. "I'm so sorry." He mouthed before trotting over to his brother.

That's it? Cassian made eye contact with Aeron who grinned at him. Aeron made it clear that he was going to keep what Leah had said to himself. Cassian pouted. He knew Leah much longer, but she continued to choose Aeron over him. It wasn't fair. He sighed and shook his head.

"Are you sure you're okay?" Cassian asked Leah.

She slowly chewed her fish and focused all of her attention on the fire. It sparked and crackled in little red and orange bursts. "I will be fine. I am going back to sleep."

Silas strutted over to them with a fiery glint in his eyes. He grabbed Leah's shirt, revealing a set of numbers on her collarbone. Cassian and Aeron shot up, and Cassian's head spun. He gripped Silas's wrist and looked up at the barrel of Silas's gun. Aeron's knife was pressed against Silas's neck.

"Ya better drop the knife or I'll shoot yer buddy in the head," Silas said to Aeron. Cassian choked back spit.

Aeron dropped the knife, and it landed with its blade in the sand. Anger flashed across his face, and his lilac eyes shimmered with rage. A muscle tensed in his neck.

"Now step back."

With a great deal of hesitation, Aeron took three steps back. His lips pressed tightly together.

"Good boy." Silas smirked.

He leered at Leah, and all thoughts ran across his face. She glared at him. The grip Cassian had on Silas's wrist tightened.

"Let go, or I'll kill ya."

"What are you going to do to her?" Anger coursed through Cassian's veins and merged with adrenaline.

"That's fer me to know." Silas pressed the gun against Cassian's head.

Leah pried Cassian's hand open. His eyes widened with shock as she pushed him out of the way. "Using me as a hostage?"

"Yer a smart girl," Silas said, releasing her shirt. He yanked her up by the arm. "It wouldn't be the first time for ya, would it?"

Leah shook her head. "It would not, but that is neither here nor there."

Leah let Silas drag her over to the campfire. Using the rope Cassian had packed, Silas bound Leah's hands, making a long lead out of the extra.

Cassian looked back at Sebastian for help. Sebastian stood across the fire. Tears reflected in the moonlight streamed down his face, but he made no indication of moving. Disappointment and rage filled him. Not just at Sebastian, but at himself. *Why am I so weak?*

"One of ya better keep watch," Silas yelled across the fire. "Ya decide, but if I see the both of ya sleeping, it's bye bye to this pretty lady."

Aeron sat beside Cassian—one leg stretched out in the sand, and the other he had bent in front of him. His gaze focused on Leah who sat on her legs directly in front of the fire with her hands tied behind her. The two of them watched the fire.

Silas grabbed Leah's hair and forced her to look into his eyes. He whispered something with a wicked glint in his eyes. He used his open hand to grab her chin.

"I am not one to bend to the will of those weaker than I," said Leah. Her voice rang clear in the night.

Aeron laughed. "Serves him right."

The slap that followed Leah's words caused Cassian to flinch, and his rage grew. Aeron stuck his hand in the sand.

Sebastian finally ran up to Silas. "Why don't we go to sleep, Silas? She'll be more cooperative in the morning."

Leah turned back to the fire. She smiled at Cassian with empty eyes. Aeron let out an odd grunt.

"I'll take the first watch," said Aeron.

"But—"

"I'll take the first watch." Aeron left no room for argument.

Cassian laid down in the sand, back facing the fire. He gritted his teeth as his tears were absorbed in the sand. *Is this what it feels like to be weak?* His heart felt as if it had sunk to the depths of the abyss and had drowned in the ocean layer. He let the exhaustion and disappointment of the day drift him into sleep.

Aeron stood up and stretched. His body screamed for sleep, but Cassian needed it more than he did. Unlocking a transcendence is said to be one of the most draining experiences of a lifetime. *I've known them for four days, and I've already grown soft.* He shook his head ruefully.

He quietly walked around the fire. Despite the late hour, it still burned. Leah tended it well as she sat in front of it. Aeron quietly laughed as she maneuvered her feet to use a stick to stir up the flames. She looked up at the sound of his voice. Dark circles graced her face.

"Is it safe? The place beyond the riverbend." Leah had said this when she first woke up earlier that evening. Aeron hadn't known what she meant, but the fear in her eyes was real. In a way, he felt the need to comfort her from her dream.

I saved this girl. Is that why I'm so upset that she's been taken hostage?

Aeron settled on the ground next to her. She scooted a little away. Her rope was staked in the sand a few feet away. It would be easy for her to escape, but she hadn't. She continued to be a mystery. She liked to act like she was disinterested in the lives of others, but there she was captive so that Cassian didn't die.

"I am tired of this," she whispered. Her eyes watched the sun come up over the horizon. She spoke as if she were talking to someone else off in the distance.

The sky was painted with gold, and the water reflected the sun in all of its majesty straight into Aeron's eyes. Thick dark clouds stormed off in the distance. They would one day make it to land, but not anytime soon. Silas snored like a grizzly bear.

"You should take Cassian and leave," whispered Leah. "It would be the best for all of us if you left."

For some reason, unknown to even Aeron, he bumped his head against hers. Her eyes widened. "Not gonna happen. You can't ditch us now. Not after all I went through to save you," he whispered close to her ear.

She sighed. "Yes, but you have a chance right now."

"I could kill both of them right now. I'd start with Silas. It would be easy." Aeron glared at Silas's curled up body.

"He is actually mostly awake. I checked moments before you walked over. At least, he stared at me when I looked at him." She monitored Cassian. His stomach was exposed, and his limbs were oddly angled. "I forgot to thank you for saving me."

"It's the first time." He rubbed the back of his neck.

Leah cocked her head. Her hair fell over her shoulder. "First time?"

"Saving a life."

Sebastian rolled over in his sleep. Leah stiffened like a board, and Aeron pulled his dagger out of its place under his shirt. Sebastian held his head protectively and curled up in a ball. With a long sigh, he relaxed and rolled back over.

"Mel said the same thing to me. Usually, you say 'you're welcome,'" Leah said. "Though I understand the sentiment. When you are trained to take lives, saving one can change your perspective on everything. Mel wanted to become a savior after she had the taste of gratitude. In a way, she did."

Aeron leaned against his arm. "Felix mentioned her once. Who is she?"

"Oh, I forgot you have not met all your siblings." Aeron knew where Leah was going. "She was your older sister, Melanthaha Sefic. She defected from the clans and was killed in the war." Leah's eyes dimmed. "She saved thousands of people as a martyr."

Aeron racked his brain for a Melanthaha. His dad had many wives, concubines, and mistresses, and many of them have children. He must've met her at least once. *Mel? Mel.*

"You fought a war?" Aeron asked, pushing away his mysterious sibling from his mind. War was much more interesting.

Leah faced him. A hardened and perfected expression painted perfectly on her face, but behind the perfection was haunting. Regret and misery lingered in the depths of her eyes and the set of her lips. "That is a story for another day. Go sleep. I will wake you before the others so you don't get in trouble."

He made a face at her. "Nope. I'll be fine."

Leah sat completely straight and still. She watched the horizon with sorrowful eyes. "If that is what you wish."

Chapter 16

whole wall of television screens projected the Trial Runners. Night had fallen on the makeshift island, and while many slept, some of the more eager Runners forged their way to the Lirith garden. Felix reclined on a red sofa in the monitoring room.

One of his personal servants brought him a meal as he watched the screen with Jin-Ae and her companions. She sat with the Sefic boy. The boy reminded Felix of Mel, and he knew Jin-Ae felt the same pain. *Jin-Ae was alway so fond of Mel. I knew she'd let that boy in.*

Jin-Ae was so much more of a person than she was three years prior when they first met. Her expression had softened. In the past, she would have sacrificed all of them for her goals. Felix was proud of the improvement and knew Wesson's son was the main reason. Two of the people she had the biggest soft spots for had, in a sense, returned to her. Felix smiled. *Please let them help her.*

Alejandro smashed a bottle against the table he was sitting at. Glass shattered everywhere. "All those years wasted. Billions of dollars and so many lives flushed down the toilet because she forgot her mission." He let out an angry shriek.

Felix fought to keep his anger in check. Jin-Ae could never escape her uncle—no, her master. In every moment, Doctor Alejandro ruled her mind. He ripped everything away from her, and it was all Felix could do not to strangle the man himself. The little girl she had once been was utterly destroyed. All documentation of her existence was gone because this man wanted to change the world.

A few of the televisions flashed off which meant one of two things: they went into the creator of the island's area, or more likely, they died. Felix ground his back teeth together. He hated this. He hated that he had to participate in it, but because of his position as leader of one of the recognized Neforian nations, he couldn't escape. Being able to watch Jin-Ae compete eased some of his discomfort. *It is sad to watch her fight for her life again.* The war didn't even distract her from saving the other living experiments.

"Alejandro, how much longer must you complain about your ludicrous experiments? How did some of your status even become one of the Trial Masters?" Duchess Elizabeth, the lovely spitfire, asked. She walked into the room with her young assistant, Friedrich, by her side.

Liz despised Alejandro. From what Felix had found out through very legal means, her husband had fallen for Alejandro's trap, and gave a large sum of money in exchange for a "gift."

Alejandro rolled his eyes. "You just don't see the changes my experiments have and will accomplish once I get her back. I will be able to unify the world with her leading my expedition to Katharnia."

Felix clenched his jaw. "What do you mean?"

With a wide grin and bloodshot eyes, Alejandro spread his arms out and did a twirl. In his white lab coat and with the scraggly beard, he looked like the mad scientist he was known to be. "It'll be perfect. I will create a perfect world just like how our precious Jin-Ae is. A world where everyone is happy, and there is no pain, no discrimination, no differences. All I need is to harness the power source of Katharnia. Did you know the power source has the ability to not only brainwash large populations, but it can also help with population control?"

Liz smacked Alejandro with her wooden cane. "It sounds like you plan mass genocide."

Alejandro waved her off. "You make it sound like it's a bad thing. Humans are always fighting for resources. If the population had been controlled better, there wouldn't be this problem. My precious Estrella would never have died if the population was better controlled and supervised."

"So you plan to sacrifice millions of people in and out of the abyss?" Felix choked out his words.

"You should be the most understanding, Supreme Leader Roman Iraklidis. If there had been one ruling government with a set of rules to choose the next leader, not only would your competitor have lived, but that Sefic girl too." Alejandro patted Felix's back. He said too much for Felix to bear. Not without Jin-Ae to grieve with him. "That girl is the blueprint for my plan. Everything I have is staked on the abilities I gave her."

In the most undignified way, Felix ran out of the room and slammed the metal door as loudly as he could. The thoughts echoed in his head along with the memories. He barely made it to his room before collapsing on the floor. It was the memories. The memories didn't fade no matter how much alcohol or drugs he consumed. The memories always came back stronger. All Felix could do was bare with them in the silence of his room.

Felix punched the floor over and over again. The screams he held back, but he let the anger and the frustration out. The pain was soothing and controllable unlike the memories. *What a way to rub salt in my wounds. No wonder so many of those idiots support him.* Alejandro would use this against him, against Jin-Ae.

Felix brought his bloodied and bruised fist to his face. *Deep breaths. Jin-Ae—no, Leah, needs someone. I need someone. Someone to save us.*

An idea lit up in his brain. He was going to help Leah as much as he could. That's what friends were for. Felix forced the sorrow down. It could control him later, but right now he had work to do. He forced himself up onto his shaky legs and booted up his laptop. Leah would need as much help in the abyss that she could get, especially if she was to save the other experiment.

He sighed. "I wish you were here, Mel. I really need you."

Chapter 17

Sebastian woke up earlier than the others, rolled over, and rummaged through his backpack which he had been using as a pillow. Silas had taken most of his medical equipment and threw it away. He was attempting to keep Sebastian safe. As a medical student, Sebastian would be a hot commodity for other Trial Runners, and Silas didn't want him to get kidnapped. The logical reasoning didn't change the fact that losing his precious tools broke Sebastian's heart. Luckily for him, Silas forgot to check the inside pocket of the backpack where Sebastian's notebook was.

The leather notebook was filled with observations of people and life around him, notes about various discussions and lectures he had attended while he was in school, and summaries of different articles he had read. Sebastian leafed through the well worn pages, skimming through the information. The last entry was about the experiments that Alejandro Perez tested. He wished Silas had let him finish the book. If he could write his thesis, it would've been on that. The main subject had been tested from the young age of ten. It was a disgusting experiment, but Sebastian was curious to see the results of such a dangerous science.

Golden light reflected off the waves and sand, casting a heavenly glow. While it was sunny with a bit of a cool breeze, dark clouds formed on the horizon. It would take a few days to get to shore, but Sebastian knew it would be a crazy storm. He could see the lightning from his spot on the sand.

Stretching, Sebastian got up from the ground and turned to wake up Silas. Whispering stopped him from completing his morning task. Leah and Aeron sat by what used to be the fire. Sebastian was genuinely surprised Aeron had stayed. Sebastian shook his head. *After watching him so desperately save Leah, I should know better. He seems like he has a kind heart.* It smoldered a little, but all signs of flames were gone. Leah was recovering way too well from drowning, but Sebastian was relieved.

Quick healing, unnatural hair, and a tattoo on the collarbone: that kind of matches up with the description of the victims of that experiment. Sebastian tapped his chin. *I'll just have to test something out.*

With a spring in his step, Sebastian walked over to Leah and Aeron. Aeron glared at him, and Leah stiffened, eyeing him suspiciously.

"What do you want?" Aeron spat out. His complexion was incredibly pale, more so than was natural at least.

He must've stayed up the whole night. Leah's not looking that much better though. "I wanted to ask something of you two."

"No." Aeron turned away.

"What do you want to ask?" Leah raised a brow. Aeron rolled his eyes, understandably still upset for being a prisoner.

Sebastian began to sweat. *If she really is an experiment, will she kill me?* He took a deep breath and strengthened his resolve. "Are you aware of Project Estrella?"

Leah's calm expression dropped and revealed a deep fear. Her lip trembled, and she bit it. His sisters had made that expression before when Silas came home drunk when Sebastian had been studying. That fear haunted them whenever Silas entered the house.

"I've heard the name before, but I couldn't tell you what it was," said Aeron.

Cassian popped up behind him, incredibly energetic for the morning. "Isn't that the weird genetic manipulation experiment where they found most of the researchers and victims murdered?"

Leah made a weird noise, drawing their attention. "Where did you learn about that?" she said in carefully enunciated Galorian.

Sebastian was curious as well. He had only heard of it recently.

"I think my dad was involved in it." Cassian looked strangely serious. There was none of his early cheer in his voice.

"No!" Leah's eyes widened. "I did not mean to say that outloud, but Wesson was not involved in it, at least not in the way you are thinking."

Cassian took a step forward. He frowned. "What do you mean?"

Leah whipped her glare to Sebastian. "I see what you are trying to do now. Thank you *very* much." She turned back to Cassian, and her expression softened. "Your father was a good man who tried his best to help when he found out what Project Estrella was."

"So are you saying you were a part of Project Estrella?" asked Aeron. He smirked as if it was some kind of joke.

Sebastian cleared his throat. "That's an odd question."

"I am Project Estrella, or more like what is left of it," said Leah. She took a large breath, and stared Sebastian in the eyes. "Sebastian was checking to see if I was one of the experiments, and his hypothesis proved true. Not only am I one of the experiments, but I am also the *blueprints.*"

The blueprints... How could I even think about bringing this up? I should've just let my curiosity stay curiosity. At least, she didn't kill me. Sebastian regretted the question now. He should've kept it to himself. Leah had gone so long with those two not knowing, and he ruined it. He always ruined things. The guilt clawed at his heart. *I was insensitive, and she's actually not okay. No one would be after that.*

There was a deep groan behind him. With a yawn, Silas slowly sat up, rubbing his jaw, and looked around. "Let's get movin'"

"Are you sure?" Sebastian asked. "We haven't had anything to eat, and you just got up."

"No time." Silas grabbed Leah's rope and tugged. "Why're ya standing there? Get movin'." He pointed to Aeron. "You take the front. I don't trust ya behind. Sebastian watch 'im."

Aeron refused to move.

"Please," Sebastian whispered.

With a battle of wills, Cassian fought to pull Aeron up. Aeron had planted himself on the ground, and while Aeron had the advantage, Cassian was winning.

"I don't want to. I'm hungry," Aeron whined.

"We can eat as we walk. Come on, Aeron. Leah's the one at risk." With one last tug, Cassian hauled Aeron to his feet.n

Leah forced herself up awkwardly, shifting her legs so that they would give her a boost. Sebastian helped her up because the lack of balance from not having access to her own arms had her tilting into the ashes from last night's fire. Her jaw clenched as she allowed him to assist her.

"Hurry up," Silas yelled. He snagged a granola bar out of Sebastian's bag. As he ate, he walked Leah away from the sand and towards the red beam of light. "We don't got all day."

Trotting behind Aeron, Sebastian observed the area. They walked on the sand, past the woods. The ocean could still be heard as they walked further and further away,

There was a striking difference in the terrain as the trees thinned out, becoming non-existent. The ground before the switch was like poorly done stitches. It wasn't a straight consistent line, but zigzagged. Sand turned into black coarse dirt. The cool breeze was replaced by a heat wave similar to when one opens the oven door, hot and dry.

Sebastian struggled to keep up. His ribs ached from walking too fast, and he breathed heavily. Sweat ran down his arms and back. *I'd much rather attend Professor Klio's chemistry class. Anything is much more pleasant than this.*

For a few miles, they trekked through the hot black sand. Sebastian grew incredibly thirsty, but there was no sign of water, or life for that matter. In the distance, he could see a ravine, but he heard no sounds of running water. Behind the ravine lived a thick forest with tall trees, creating a canopy under their large leaves. The red beam laid past the forest.

It'll take us at least a day to get through this horrible part.

Leah had been tripped by Silas three times which slowed down their pace. Sebastian pitied her, but the breaks taken to pull her off the ground were needed. Aeron looked murderous each time they stopped. *Was it because they were stopping or Leah?*

At one point, Aeron stretched out an arm. An animal passed in front of them. Sebastian had a hard time determining whether it was truly an animal or not. It was humongous and ball shaped. It rolled in front of Aeron. All of its inner contents could be seen through its clear flash. Its body billowed underneath itself and brushed up against Aeron's face and shirt. It continued to move away, but it left Aeron's shirt wet.

Cassian gawked at the creature. "What is that?" He whispered to Sebastian.

"I've got no idea, but it is certainly an odd creature." Sebastian smiled. "It looks like a water bed."

"For real." Cassian laughed.

"Ya could've fought that," Silas complained.

Ignoring the comment, Aeron continued to make his way to the ravine. Silas mumbled under his breath about, "nobody respecting his authority." To Sebastian's relief, that was all Silas did.

Thunder rolled in the distance, and a large group of clouds formed behind them. Lightning flashed underneath the clouds. Aeron picked up the pace, and Sebastian's ribs screamed.

"What're ya doing? Move girl," Silas shrieked.

Sebastian turned. Cassian was trying to get her to move, and Silas was yelling in her face. Leah's entire focus was on the storm. She jumped when it thundered again.

"Come on, Leah," said Cassian. "The faster we move, the faster we'll get to a shelter and can wait out the storm. It'll be okay. I promise."

Leah nodded. A haunting lingered in her eyes. *Poor girl. So much haunts her. I could never be as strong as she is.*

Nothing else occurred as they walked to the ravine besides a very sad lunch break. All of the granola bars Sebastian had packed in case of emergencies were devoured. The storm slowly grew closer, but it wouldn't reach them until that night at the earliest.

The ravine wasn't incredibly wide, but too wide for Leah to jump across tied up and Sebastian to ever jump over. He really needed to get back in shape. The ravine was deep and had an eerie darkness about it.

"Please untie Leah," Cassian said to Silas. "It'll be easier for her to get across."

"I refuse." Silas grinned with a wild look in his eyes.

Cassian fumbled for words. Sebastian was surprised that Aeron hadn't moved from the ravine. *Is he really not concerned for her?*

As if reading his thoughts, Leah winked at Sebastian. She had a weird smirk on her face. "Do not worry, Cassian." The rope snapped. It was frayed like she had been sawing at it. Blood dripped into the black dirt, and large slits on her wrists sealed back together. Her rope burns faded as she held up Aeron's dagger. "Silas was too busy watching other things on me that he did not catch the weird way I was rubbing my arms together."

Sebastian let out an amazed laugh. "Amazing. Is that why you two were hanging out this morning?" He paled. "Oh my goodness, you've been bleeding out all day! How are you standing? You also almost drowned yesterday."

Leah shrugged. Her back turned to Silas.

"Watch out!" Aeron yelled behind Sebastian as Silas lunged at Leah.

Cassian pushed her out of the way, getting dogpiled by Silas in her stead. Leah quickly got up off the ground, and Aeron raced to their side. He looked ready to hop in as they wrestled against each other in the dirt. Silas had the upper hand with his hands around Cassian's neck. Cassian kneed Silas in the gut and pushed him off, trying to get up. They stood too close to the ravine, and Silas noticed. Sebastian saw him eyeing the ravine.

"Silas, no." Sebastian ran to stop him.

Silas pushed Cassian over the edge and laughed. Sebastian looked over the edge, shaking in fear. Cassian was holding on to dear life. Somehow, he had caught a small ledge, but his arms were shaking, and fingers slipping. Aeron sidled up next to Sebastian, reaching for Cassian.

"So yer siding with them," said Silas. "Ya rather save yer buddy than yer brotha. I shoulda just left ya. Who'd knew ya be so useless."

Silas stomped on Sebastian's back over and over again. Tears leaked from his eyes. "Cassian, you're going to have to let go with one hand and reach."

Cassian looked at him, fear in his eyes. With a firm nod, Cassian showed where his trust laid. He swung his arm up, losing balance with the other arm. He missed Aeron's hand, and began to fall.

Sebastian lunged for his hand. Cassian's fingers almost slipped from his grasp. He wrapped his other hand around Cassian's wrist. All of his weight bore down on Sebastian. His arms shook as he tried to lift Cassian out. The stomping had stopped. Aeron reached over and grabbed Cassian as well. The two of them awkwardly heaved him out.

Once he was out of the ravine, Cassian crawled as far away as possible. He took shaky breaths. "That was scary."

Sebastian nodded in agreement. His heart raced in his chest, his arms and back hurt, and he really wanted a nap. *Where's Silas?*

"You okay?" asked Aeron, heading to Leah.

She stood over Silas. The world was quiet and numb. *Why is Silas on the ground?* Aeron's dagger dripped with blood. Droplet after droplet hit the ground. Aeron rested a hand on Leah's trembling shoulder. Cassian looked up at Leah and Aeron. With wide eyes, Cassian looked back at Sebastian.

"Sebastian," Cassian said.

"It's—it's okay." Tears streamed down Sebastian's face. "She reacted accordingly to the situation. He was trying to prevent us from saving you. He was honestly a horrible person. He lied, cheated, and harmed others. So why am I crying? He got what he deserved, but it hurts so much. He caused me so much pain, but I feel like my heart is being ripped from my chest. Why is that?"

Cassian crawled over to Sebastian, and put an arm around his shoulder. Sebastian sobbed and sobbed. Instead of being mad at him, they waited patiently, and instead of being mad at Leah, there was relief. *Silas cannot do anything now. He can still be the child I remembered him as.* He hiccuped. *I should've been a better brother. I'm sorry, Silas.*

For all the berating she did to Cassian for being glued to the television, Amyra hadn't left it for days. She got her meals delivered to her small hotel room. If she needed to go out, she streamed it on her phone. As long as her kids were in the Trials, Amyra would be watching.

Her heart had practically stopped numerous times. She should've never let them go. They would be safe and sound if she hadn't. Cassian and Leah would never have stayed even if she banned them from going. Cassian was just as stubborn as his father had been, and Leah was driven by some mysterious goal.

Amyra was once again drawn into the television, watching her children and their friends jump over a ravine. The new one, a sweet looking boy from one of the free villages, fell a little short, and Cassian, Leah, and Aeron ran over to catch him. Aeron laughed as they tumbled into a pile.

Someone knocked on her door, and reluctantly she got up. Amyra brushed her hair down and practiced her smile before opening the door. "Yes?"

A beautiful man with deep blue eyes walked into her room without invitation. He forced the door closed and locked it. He eyed the television before sitting on her unmade bed. Amyra stood there with her mouth agape.

"Young man," she started.

"Supreme Ruler Roman Iraklidis of the Neforian country of Quita at your service." He gave her a little head nod. Amyra stumbled against the door. "Do you mind if I turn my disguise off?"

When she didn't respond, Roman turned it off anyway, revealing a young boy, maybe the same age as Cassian. Amyra suspected he was a bit younger. His blue eyes remained the same, but in the place of his blond hair, he had black. Instead of his perfectly smooth, tanned skin, he was pale as if he had never seen the sun, and a horrible burn ruined half of his face. "This is the first time in months that I've taken that off."

Amyra nodded awkwardly. "Is that so?"

Roman pulled out a notebook. "Now on to business. My best friend, Leah, has been in your care for a year and a half now, am I right?"

"Yes?"

"Do you have any emotional attachment to her?" Roman asked, pen ready.

"Of course I do. She is like my own child." Amrya placed her hands on her hips. "What does this have to do with anything?"

Roman looked up to her. His expression was incredibly grim. "I fear she's in grave danger."

Chapter 18

ounding ahead of the others, Leah enjoyed being free from the ropes. She tried to keep her mind off the incoming storm, but the rolling thunder grew closer with each passing minute. Sebastian avoided her since the ravine, and while it saddened her a little, she understood. She pushed down all of those sappy and useless feelings into her box. *I don't know how much more it can take. Why did I kill him? He could've been easily captured.*

She forged her way through the trees, but they all looked the same. Using Aeron's knife, Leah marked one of the trees with her numbers. It was the easiest thing for her to remember. Cassian consoled Sebastian as they walked. His voice came out as a whisper, and though she couldn't hear his words, she was comforted to know he was there. *I've grown too weak.*

"Is it just me or are we going in circles?" asked Aeron.

Leah nodded. Sebastian and Cassian looked around wildly.

"We should split up and see if we all come back here," Leah suggested. The storm was coming closer, and she needed to get away from them. The wind started to catch up with them, and the trees bent in the wind.

"There's absolutely no way that's gonna happen," said Cassian. "You're dumb to think we'd let anyone go along with this weather coming. Oh."

Leah glared at him, and Aeron raised his brows. "We should look for shelter then. Plus it's getting pretty dark."

"I am down for shelter," said Sebastian as he eyed the trees.

With their conclusions, Leah led the way. They came to her marked tree over and over again. At one point, she thought she found her way out of the loop. It only ended up being the other side of her marked tree.

A black fox ran in front of her. The first change in hours. It blended in with the shadows, but every once in a while, it would let out a horrid scream like sound. A boom of thunder rang around them, and Leah's heart began to race.

Aeron raced after the fox. Cassian kept up with him easily, but Leah and Sebastian casually walked. Her heart raced in her chest, and she felt as if there were hands grabbing her arms, legs, and neck. The feeling moved to her chest and back. *Why are there so many hands? Always hands.*

They were led onto an old, but well worn path. Aeron cheered. Something ran up Leah's leg, and she squealed. Cassian grabbed her hand and gave it a comforting squeeze, but her mind was already being overtaken. Thunder, rain, and lightning decided to join up with Leah and the others, encasing them in a harsh torrent.

The storm raged around them as they forged their way through the forest. Leah forced herself to keep moving as the roaring wind pushed against her. Cold rain pelted her skin. Leah's head ached from the change in weather, and she couldn't catch her breath. Chills ran up and down her spine.

Thunder rumbled menacingly, and the memories rolled in with them. Lightning struck in their general vicinity. Leah stumbled. The noises were growing louder and louder. Cassian walked beside her, quietly enjoying the rain despite the nip of the air and electric pulse, while Aeron and Sebastian ran ahead, searching for shelter.

Cassian spoke to her, but his voice was overwhelmed by the screaming. Leah searched for the owner of the scream, but the only ones around were Cassian, Aeron, and Sebastian. Lightning struck again, leaving its scorched mark on the world and in her head.

Without a second thought, Leah bolted through the trees. She thought she saw Cassian follow, but only shadows chased her. Like a beast, she clawed her way through the underbrush. Her body tensed at any sound and movement, but when lightning struck she stilled. Something crashed behind her. It trampled through the trees, yelling her name. Their voices were so familiar, but not. They knew her, but she couldn't remember who they were. Her heartbeat sped up even faster, and the cold air in her lungs burned.

It was all in her head. Leah had been stuck in her head for so long. She never wanted to be this way. *Why did this have to happen to me?* She tripped on a tree root, but another roar of thunder sent her running through the woods.

I wish it had been me. Years ago, Leah had wished for happiness. It had been her greatest desire as it was to many, but that was stripped away from her. Death would erase her sins—pay for her sins—and the nightmares that plagued her every moment would drift into nothingness. She wanted nothingness, at least that is what she told herself. A small part of her longed for things of the past, but the past was gone. The past only left her one option, but not until she saved Alayna.

Was happiness too much to ask for? Are my sins even forgivable?

Can someone accept the blood that stained her hands?

No. Leah knew she was too far gone. Her lungs hungered for air, and her mind begged for a reprieve. Tears blurred her vision as they melded with the rain. She stood completely alone. No trees protected her. No bush hid her. She was out in an open field, alone as she always had been. An arc of lightning struck the ground a few yards away, inciting a scream. A warning peal of thunder echoed around her head.

Her uncle's laughter reverberated against the walls as she begged for mercy. Leah was back in that room: the white walls, the horrible stench of antiseptic, and the hands poking and prodding her. Electricity ran through her body as she fought to break from the bindings of that cold metal chair.

No, no, no...

Leah dropped to her knees. The box of emotions threatened to break open.

It can't be real. It isn't real... She tried to convince herself. *How could it not be real?*

Water dripped through the leaves and bounced off her skin in hard bullets. She dug her fingers into her arms. The pain was a clear reminder that she was free.

My dear Jin-Ae, how could you be free? I'm still here, aren't I? You know what that means. You'll never be free.

The box she had so carefully crafted broke. The contents spilled out, and Leah desperately shoved them back in. It was no use. Once released, there was no putting them back in. The box was completely broken, and the torrent of emotions, of sensations, of wretched memories, overwhelmed her. If the lightning didn't kill her, this would. *Maybe it's better this way...*

Muffled voices surrounded her. They were the ones from her darkest nightmares and most vivid memories, the ones she wanted to forget the most. More needles, more DNA rewriting. Something went wrong. Bodies, dead bodies. The smell of rotting flesh. The electricity ran up her skin, soaking into her bones. Laughter, but not her own. Thunder rumbled and left scars. Blood puddled around her. She could see their bodies. All of their bodies. She stared at her bloodied hands.

Alayna. Where was Alayna? She wasn't ready. They couldn't sell her off. Don't touch her! Leave them alone. Bodies, so many bodies. Ah, Leah was all alone again. Thunder. Screams. Bodies. Injections. *Where was Alayna?*

Why couldn't she save them?

Arms surrounded her. The comfort in their warmth startled Leah. The memories in her mind dimmed. She could control these. Her screams quieted into little whimpers and her sobs slowed. She buried her head into Cassian's shoulder. His woodsy scent scared away the smell of rotting flesh and blood. He rubbed her back. Warm... like fresh blood. She flinched away, pushing him far from her, from the blood, from the monster she was.

He grabbed her hands and whispered, but her mind had not been silenced. Slowly, he pulled her back. She felt the rumbling in his chest, but couldn't hear his voice. She watched Aeron sit beside her. Genuine concern glazed his eyes. He held one of her freezing hands. He rubbed his thumb along her wrist before squeezing it. Leah laced their fingers together, absorbing his warmth too. His brows furrowed, but he didn't let go. If she was dreaming, she refused to wake up.

Cassian and Aeron spoke over her head, yelling over the storm. The rain became significantly worse, but so did her anxiety. She buried herself as far into her brother as she could. Aeron let go of her hand. Cassian pulled away and Leah cried out. He pet her head as Aeron picked her up. She situated herself so that he was holding her like a child. She put her head in the crook of his neck. Her sobbing came back in full as the lightning and thunder increased.

"You need to find Sebastian fast," Aeron said. "He seems resourceful enough to find shelter."

She couldn't hear Cassian's response. She couldn't hear anything over the screaming.

"It's too loud," she cried. "It's too loud."

She desperately struggled out of Aeron's arms. He let her down and crouched on the ground. They were eye-level.

"Aeron, I can't—it's too loud. I—" Hiccups joined her sobbing. She spoke purely in Livithian. "They're still screaming! Always screaming... I'm tired of the screaming and the pain. When will this be over?"

Aeron covered her ears. His eyebrows furrowed as he comforted her as best as he could. The screaming quieted briefly.

"You... you are not at fault," he said.

She sniffled. "I killed them. I caused their suffering. If only it had been me. I wish it had been me. Why? Why?"

He turned away briefly. He nodded at something in the distance. Gently, he helped her up. Her legs refused to hold her up so Aeron picked her up. The only thing keeping her in the present was the beat of

Aeron's heart through his shirt. He rocked back and forth, as the rain pelted them before moving out of the field. His steady pace and heart beat calmed her mind. Was she allowed to rely on anybody anymore? Before her brain could answer itself, Aeron lulled her to sleep.

Heavy weight settled into Leah's side as Cassian completely relaxed on her shoulder. Something covered her arms, keeping her warm. Her back ached from sitting on stone all night long. Reluctantly, she forced her sleep crusted eyes open. The memories of the storm flashed into her mind, and she wanted to throw herself off a cliff.

Cassian's hair fell over his eyes. His breath came in heavy and a slight snore escaped his lips. He shifted so his back rested on her side. The cold breeze from the cave's entrance was blocked from Leah. His body shielded her from the elements.

Across the floor, Sebastian slept. His glasses rested next to him. In his sleep, he looked younger than Cassian. Leah suspected that wasn't the case. He stirred in his sleep, rolling onto his side. The rock he rested on looked anything but comfortable.

Aeron's jacket was tucked around her protectively. She looked up at the boy who she had been using as a headrest. He side-eyed her before turning away with a blush creeping across his face. He leaned against a large rock, seemingly trying to escape being her pillow, but feeling too guilty to move across the area.

A smirk settled onto Leah's lips as the boy poorly tried to feign indifference. "Thank you," she said. Her voice was thick from sleep.

The blush made its way down the pale boy's neck. "What—what are you talking about?"

"The jacket."

"It's not what you think." He refused to look at her.

Her smirk grew into a grin, and she wrapped the jacket closer to her. "But I do appreciate it. It was very... very kind of you." Leah grimaced at her inability to remember the right Galorin word.

Aeron nodded. Unsatisfied with his response, she pulled one arm out of its warm protection. She grabbed his chin like her mom would do when Leah was refusing to listen. His lilac eyes widened.

"Listen. When I thank you, you accept. When you do something nice, you get rewarded," she scolded in her first language. It flowed off her tongue like water, smooth and flowery. Using it made her miss her home. "I refuse to let my friends treat themselves badly."

"I—we're friends?"

Leah let his chin go and nestled closer to Cassian. Cassian's head fell onto her ribs as she moved. She sucked in her pain, afraid that letting out any signs of pain would wake him. "Yes. I am tired of pretending that I hate you."

This soft spot I have for Mel is annoying, but she loved Aeron. Even if he cannot remember her. He is exactly as she told me.

Aeron's confused, but excited grin, warmed her heart. *If only Mel could see this.* Cassian stirred, hitting the top of her head when he stretched. He bounced into a sitting position, way too awake for someone who just woke up. He bear-hugged Leah and Aeron. Aeron made a weird noise from the back of his throat. Cassian laughed at Aeron's embarrassment. Leah let herself enjoy their warmth.

"I was so worried. Please, never do that again," Cassian scolded Leah. His brow creased with concern. "I thought you'd never come back. You scared me."

She looked at her feet, trying to figure out an appropriate answer.

Sebastian sat up and put on his glasses. "It was quite terrifying. I wish I could've been more helpful."

"You found the shelter, correct?" asked Leah. Sebastian gave a curt nod. "Then you helped tremendously. I would be in an unhealthy state if you had not used your skills to find a place to rest."

Sebastian gave her a small smile. "If you say so."

"Anyhow, what caused you to freak out so bad?" Aeron asked.

"I—I am afraid of lightning," she said, embarrassed by the confession. "When I was displeasing, he would electrocute me and my companions. My mind always associates thunder and lightning, so I panicked. I am sorry."

Warm arms surrounded Leah. Cassian squeezed her tight. "You've got nothing to be sorry for."

"It isn't even your fault," added Sebastian. "You were just a child."

They can not imagine what I have done. If they knew, they would abandon me. Especially Cassian, if he found out what happened with Wesson... I have to keep that away from him. It is for the best. This has always been for the best.

Tears streamed down from her eyes, leaking onto his shirt. "You do not understand. Even you would not be able to forgive me. I am a monster."

Aeron laughed. "If you're a monster, what does that make me? I kill people for a living."

"A caged bird," she said. Leah moved away from Cassian and wiped her eyes. All of Aeron's laughter left his eyes.

The silence was suffocating, and Leah wished she had chosen her words differently, but the grip the Sefic family had on their children was scary, and Aeron's mother was the worst of them all.

Cassian cleared his voice. "Anyway, what we're trying to say is that you're not as bad as you think you are. You shouldn't have had to go through such an experience. No one should. Plus, like Sebastian said, you were just a kid. Those things you were forced to do don't reflect badly on you."

Leah shook her head. "You are not understanding,"

"How am I supposed to understand when you won't clarify?" Cassian snapped, causing Leah to flinch. His eyes widened.

Aeron stood up and brushed off his pants. "We better get moving. Time is ticking away."

Leah followed him as he walked out of the cave. "Aeron—"

"Nope, don't say it." He laughed. "I was just shocked at how accurate that description was. We know each other, right? From before this. Did you know who Cassian was when you started living with him and his mom?"

Despite the thick clouds that covered the sky, the forest was alive. A rabbit scampered out of a bush and munched on some berries. A bird swooped down from a nearby tree to pick at a bug. Stalking the rabbit, a black fox crossed Leah and Aeron's path. It chittered at them before running after its prey.

"I knew both of you," she said. *I wish I did not. I wish those days never happened.*

Aeron whipped around. His purple eyes lit with emotion. "Then why can't I remember?"

"You knew me before?" asked Cassian from behind Leah. She jumped. His mouth was dangling open.

Sebastian stretched in the mouth of the cave. His glasses were falling off his nose, and a tear formed on the knees of his pants.

"It would be for the best that you stop thinking about it. There is a reason you cannot remember." Leah shivered.

I wish I could forget.

Birds shot out of their hiding places among the leaves as a blood curdling scream pierced the air. A deep booming roar accompanied the flight of birds. A woman ran through the trees, weaving around them as she fled. The ground rumbled. Trees cracked and fell to the ground. Leah could have sworn she saw fire over the trees.

Than ran through the forest after the woman. Behind him was a large black dragon with golden eyes like the sun. Smoke billowed out of its mouth, and it let out another roar. Leah felt it rumbling in her chest.

The woman tripped in the dragon's path. Its large claw landed on her body, and the crunch of her bones was nauseating. The dragon continued on its pursuit of Than. It caught sight of Sebastian, and its golden eyes narrowed.

"I think this is when we start running," Sebastian said with a shaky voice.

Chapter 19

Trees whirled past Aeron's vision as he sprinted behind Sebastian. Running was useless though. Weaving through the forest slowed them down, but the dragon plowed after them, knocking tree after tree down. It fixated its attention to Sebastian, forgetting about Than.

With super thick legs, the dragon stomped on the underbrush. The black fox they'd seen earlier screamed at it and bared its teeth. In the daytime, the dragon stuck out like a sore thumb, but Aeron could imagine what a nightmare it would be at night. The scales reflected light in a way that would create excellent camouflage across the skies and under the stars.

Exertion hit Aeron full for as he ran, slowing him down substantially. He was surprised he made it this long with so little sleep. His legs began to tremble, but he forced a smirk on his face. *They'll be unnecessarily worried if they notice how tired I am. Wait—why would they even worry about me?* A claw landed next to him. Aeron jumped away from the ivory nails and black scales. *I'll ponder over this later.*

Leah and Cassian ran ahead of him and Sebastian, catching up with Than. They tried to steer clear of him, but their twist and turning left them running next to him. He sneered at Leah. She returned the expression with her own unfriendly gesture.

If the dragon wanted, it could torch them. They were only a claws length away. It roared and made a lot of noise but never attacked. The dragon chased, but never caused any physical harm. It was trying to scare them. A puff of smoke billowed from its leathery lips.

Like cattle being rounded up by a rancher, they were herded into the meadow that Leah had been found in. Sebastian stopped running and cradled his left arm. A light broke through his shirt sleeve. He forced his sleeve up, revealing a large swirling and glowing black tattoo.

"Is that a transcendence?" asked Aeron, stepping between Sebastian and the dragon. He couldn't hold the dragon off, but at least he could give Sebastian a chance to run. Sebastian panted, shaking his head.

The dragon stopped right before the two of them. The sulfur smell filled Aeron's nostrils and made his stomach churn. He covered his nose.

"Aeron, Sebastian!" Cassian yelled for them. He was in the middle of the field. Leah and Than stood nearby, arguing.

Pushing Aeron aside, the dragon forced its way to Sebastian. Its black scales reflected the morning sun straight into Aeron's eyes. It purred and poked Sebastian with its snout. The heat radiating off its body made Aeron sick.

"It should be okay. I don't think it'll attack. I have a dragon kin's blessing." Sebastian said. He rubbed one of the giant black scales with trembling fingers. "I think that man over there startled the dragon. I can feel its confusion and concern."

Aeron gave the dragon a pat. Its body was almost too hot to touch. "It seems friendly. Do you think it'll let us ride it?"

"No." Sebastian laughed. "Though that would be really neat. Where's Leah and Cass?"

Leah's pained screams, a sound that had grown so familiar, startled Aeron. He turned around as shadowy black flames encased her body and absorbed into her skin. Than stood there smugly as his transcendence began to course through her veins. A satisfied look settled on his face.

"Leah?" Sebastian ran towards her. The dragon galloped behind him like a puppy, eventually overtaking him, and got to Leah before him.

I should've killed him much earlier. Aeron quietly made his way through the meadow. His brother was completely sucked up in his "victory" and the dragon. *This will be easy.* He pulled out his dagger from underneath his shirt.

Taking Than unaware, Cassian punched him in the jaw. Than's concentration faltered, and the shadows pooled out of Leah's skin and made its way to Than's shadow. The dragon roared, and with the warning, Than started to slip into his shadow. Cassian grabbed Than's greasy hair, and pulled him all the way out of the shadow.

Aeron arrived next to Cassian. Than created a shadow wall, and Cassian was forced to let go as it burned into his skin. Throwing his dagger in the shadows, Aeron heard a satisfying yelp. A shadow puddle was left where Than had been standing. It slithered away like a snake.

His original intent was to keep his transcendence hidden, but seeing the shadow slither away after hurting his friend, Aeron kind of lost track of himself. Snapping his fingers, a great fireball formed over his head. He flicked it at the shadow which screamed and screamed, slithering away as fast as it could to the safety of water.

Sebastian had a hand on Leah's back. She shook violently. "Why is it always me? When will these punishments end?"

Aeron's words caught in his throat.

"Are you alright? Are you hurt anywhere?" asked Cassian as he walked in front of her. She had her head in her hands.

Leah looked up at no one in particular. The whites of her eyes were as black as the dragon's scales, but they didn't shine. Cassian gasped. Carefully, she felt her face and covered her eyes. A choking noise escaped her lips.

I'm going to kill him. I'm going to make him wish he'd never been born. There was no way this wasn't his fault.

"I am quite frightened," she said, trying to laugh.

Sebastian examined her eyes. "It's like there's a film over your eyes. I'm honestly not sure what is happening to them. I'm so sorry, Leah."

"I thought things were getting better, but I should have known. There is no need for you to apologize for it. I was the one who let my guard down." Leah forced a brave face, and something twinged in Aeron's chest. "We should get moving."

Leah took a shaky step forward, and then another. "Sebastian, the dragon is a red flag. You should do something about it."

"We should let you rest," said Cassian, grabbing her shoulders as she stumbled.

She brushed him off, trying to walk on her own. "And what good would that do? My eyesight won't come back, and neither will the lost time." Leah began walking before turning around. "Where is the light again?"

This idiot. Aeron walked over to her. "Stop pretending to be strong," he whispered.

"I am not doing it for you," Leah said. "Now lead me to the gardens.

I would like to get out of here and into a shower."

Aeron laughed while Cassian and Sebastian wore miserable expressions. Cassian hooked his arm around Leah's, and he led her through the forest. They traveled down the same path as the night before. There were no signs of the fox that had guided them.

Sebastian was telling Cassian about the masters program he was attending when the world around them shimmered. Aeron groaned. *Why does this keep happening to us? Why can't we travel in peace? I just want to go to the garden and take a nao.* Leah grabbed his arm. She was swaying.

The shimmering stopped. The forest was gone, and in its place were large ruins. It was at least three stories tall with large spiral towers at each corner. Stone gargoyles protected the roof, and stone lions guarded the entrance. Bricks had fallen out of the wall and vines crawled up the stones. A large tree grew from the middle of the temple.

Aeron felt drawn to go in. A pull so overwhelming, he could not resist. Leah clung hard to his arm and brought him back. Without realizing it, he walked up to the entrance. Cassian bounded off ahead of him.

"Ruins," he said. Excitement glittered in Cassian's eyes. All concern blown away by curiosity. "Let's go in! It'll be like we're real adventurers."

"And what would you call all our other adventures to this point?" Aeron's voice raised an octave. Leah chuckled under her breath.

Sebastian opened and closed his mouth. He itched to speak but something held his words back.

Cassian ran back to Sebastian. "What do you think?"

"If you have something to say, then say it." Aeron smirked.

Fear flashed in Sebastian's eyes. "It's—it's nothing."

Cass frowned. "You sure? If something's bothering you, we'll back off."

Sebastian eyed them suspiciously. "You won't like it."

Aeron groaned. "Just say it."

"Be kind." Leah pinched his cheek.

Cass nodded. "Yeah, Aeron. What if I rushed you when you bathed, how would you feel?"

Sebastian rolled his eyes and took a deep breath. "I have a bad feeling. Like I want to go in, but the feeling isn't from me. I think we should figure a way out."

His feelings were correct, Aeron noted as the ground beneath them collapsed. He moved Leah to his front so that he could cover her from debris. Cass screamed like a little girl.

They seemed to fall forever. Aeron got bored.

Chapter 20

Hard earth underneath her and darkness around her, Leah rolled onto her stomach. Every inch of her body hurt, and she felt a rib heal itself. Her fingers ran against warm flesh. Calloused hands enveloped hers. Heavy breathing echoed wherever they were at. Leah's back and lungs ached from hitting the ground. Water dropped in puddles nearby. Something above head flapped its wings.

The hands tugged her up into a sitting position before hugging her. Cassian sniffled. He rested his cheek against hers, getting them both wet with his tears. She let his warmth flow through her, pushing away some of the fear. Not being able to see bothered her. Her other senses heightened to make up for the loss, but not enough.

Leah heard rustling next to her and reached out. Her hand pressed into fabric and hard stomach. The person moved swiftly away.

"Shrimp, if you would refrain," Aeron said in a smug voice. She reached back over and pinched him. He slapped her hands away, and shuffled to the other side of the area. He knocked on rock before swearing.

Cassian helped her up onto her feet. Dust filled her nostrils and without her hands, she ended up sneezing all over her brother. Metal clanged against the stone floor.

"Oops," Sebastian laughed. "My hand slipped. Does anyone else want a flashlight? I have two."

"I'll take one," Cassian said.

Leah felt her way around the room. Rocks littered the ground, making her trip more times than she'd like to admit. One of the stones bounced off another object which Leah quickly found out was the wall. Her nose smacked into jagged rock, and she feared it would bleed. Her hands shook.

"I can't find the door," she said. "I can't find anything actually."

Aeron snorted. "What? You don't have echolocation like the rest of us?"

"Your comments are not helpful, not that you've been useful to begin with."

"Hey! That is uncalled for." Aeron laughed as he banged his knuckles against the wall. He had a hearty laugh that came from deep inside his chest. "I think the only way out is up. Unless one of you can find a weak spot."

Leah figured she could look—feel—for an exit. Someone shuffled next to her and tapped on her shoulder. Slowly, she turned.

"It would be better if you stayed close to one of us," said Sebastian. His voice was rich and deep like hot chocolate. Leah nodded and grabbed his wrist. She could feel the blood flowing through his veins.

The ground shook and the earth rumbled. Sebastian wrapped his arms around Leah, causing her to stiffen. Her body was tense. She locked her jaw. Everything continued to shake, and Leah, who couldn't see, felt nauseous. Her mind couldn't connect to her body. A rock fell and hit her shoulder. It hurt.

Sebastian covered her head. Leah heard scraping across the room like a door opening for the first time in many years. Aeron yelped in surprise, and footsteps ran towards the noise.

Holding her hand, Sebastian led Leah to the others. A cold and musty breeze hit Leah's face. She scrunched her nose. The smell of decaying plants and animals wafted out from the doorway.

Sebastian leaned next to Leah's head. "It's a tunnel," he whispered.

Leah nodded. She was grateful that Sebastian was not making a big deal out of her disability. She was already weak. Weaker than she was ever meant to be. Even her uncle messed up with her. With all his experimenting, he couldn't change the fact that she was useless. A waste of existence.

She shook the thoughts out, or at least tried to. Her mind wandered back to those thoughts. Always back to the past. The darkness brought out the worst in people. They get away with so much in the dark. Thoughts worked the same way. They did the most harm when you can't see the light.

"Whoever finds the exit first wins," Aeron whispered loudly.

Cassian laughed. "That sounds like a horrible idea, but why not?"

Their feet pattered farther and farther away, leaving Leah with a stranger. Sebastian guided her. He helped her over rocks and under branches, though the branches were too tall for Leah to bother with. Sebastian whistled quietly. His hand shook in hers.

Water ran through what Leah assumed were cracks in the walls. It would only make sense since so much wildlife grew on the floor. Grass and weeds rubbed against her ankles. Roots tripped her and small animals scurried by her head and feet.

More scraping echoed ahead of them. Cassian whooped. Leah used his cackling to navigate more by herself. Sebastian refused to let her go. He continued to guide her despite her desire for independence. She mumbled under her breath. They came to an abrupt stop. She knocked a few pebbles loose as she shuffled to stabilize herself. The pebbles hit the ground far below them.

"There's a chasm. It isn't super wide but it seems pretty deep," Sebastian said. "Cassian, you should come here. I can't help her."

A running start landed Cassian next to her. He wrapped her arms around his neck and picked her up piggyback style. She groaned. "Do you have to?"

"Sorry."

"You don't sound sorry."

Cassian laughed and walked backwards. He took off running. Her grip tightened and she squeezed her eyes shut. He left the ground and they began to fall.

"I thought you said it was not wide," Leah said, before she started swearing in her native language.

His feet hit the ground, jolting her from the impact. He tilted back in the direction of the chasm. A hand gripped her arm, pulling them forward. They toppled over Aeron who swore in Galorian and earned a whack from Leah.

"This is how you thank me? With a smack? Shrimp, maybe you should learn how to be grateful." Aeron wheezed.

Sebastian helped her off of the boys. "Are you alright? Do you have any pain?"

"I am doing fine," she said. "Elikar, if you say naughty things in front of Cassian one more time, I will end you. He has innocent ears. Let us go, Sebastian.”

“I do not,” said Cassian as let her down.

She landed on a really soft stone. *I wonder if it's moss.*

Her foot caught on one of the obnoxious tree roots. She skidded on some mossy cobblestone. Blood seeped out of her newly injured knee before healing up. Nausea raised into her throat, and she forced herself back on her feet despite the pounding in her head. Aeron shuffled next to her, clothes rustling against each other.

Leah grabbed his shirt to keep him still to end him, not because her knees buckled. He stilled. “Caught you,” she said with a shaky voice. “Stop running around like an idiot. What if something popped out?”

“You did that on purpose? I was actually wo—” He let her pull him down to her level. “Ow. Don’t pinch my cheeks that hard. What if you ruined my awe-inspiring good looks?”

Cassian walked behind her. His footsteps were heavy as he trudged through undergrowth. Sebastian walked quietly, almost timidly, as if he was afraid of being caught. They grabbed her arms and dragged her away from Aeron.

“Leah, you can’t attack Aeron like that. He’s too weak to defend him- self,” Cassian said. He forced her to move further into the ruins.

“I’m too what?” Aeron’s voice raised an octave.

Sebastian sighed. “You don’t have to deny it. That’s why you keep your distance. You don’t have the strength for close ranged attacks.”

Aeron stomped around them and led the group. “I’ll show you.”

Cassian patted Leah’s hand. “Don’t worry. He is a bit sensitive.”

“Sensitive? I’m sensitive?” He screamed in fake anguish, or maybe real. Leah could hear his scream over the rumbling of the ruins.

The ground shifted beneath them. Cassian stood firm and Leah used him as support. She bent down, holding onto Cassian's leg, and tried to keep her motion sickness down. It only made it worse. She threw up. Stomach acid raced out of her mouth like a hose.

Tree branches creaked overhead. Cassian grabbed her and shoved her out of the way. She threw up again from the motion. Wood cracked against the stone next to her head, and a branch shot past her nose. Cassian helped her to her feet. The branches creaked and cracked as they swooshed around Leah.

"You need to get on my back," Cassian said. Urgency and panic filled his voice. Leah protested. "Right now!"

She slipped onto his back without another word. Cassian took off running.

"Did you set off a booby trap?" asked Cassian once he caught up with the others.

Cassian jumped to the side. Wind rustled her hair as another branch flew by. Frustration ate at her. If only she could see...

"I think we're being herded somewhere," Sebastian called out. "Let's head for it. Maybe the trees will leave us alone."

"I like your style. Go where the enemy is." Aeron cackled.

Cassian changed directions and charged ahead. Something fell on Leah's back. It moved, heading towards her head. Its tongue flicked at the back of her neck. She swallowed hard. The snake slithered across her bare neck. It was quite cold against her skin.

"Cassian, I do hope you aren't afraid of snakes." She kept her body as still as possible as it slithered around her neck.

"I'm not."

She relaxed a tiny bit. "Good because it is slithering next to your face."

Cassian turned his head. His hair tickled her nose. "How do you know that?" The snake made its way down her arm. It rubbed its scales on Cassian's cheek. "Oh, that's why."

He jumped over an object. The snake fell off her arm and Cassian sped up.

"I see something at the end of this hallway," Sebastian said. "Maybe it's the exit."

"That would be boring," Aeron whined. "I want to fight something."

Leah scoffed. "When do you not want to fight something?"

"Probably in his sleep." Cassian slowed his run. The branches stopped hitting her head and arms. "That's so weird."

Leah opened her mouth to ask what he meant was weird. However, she felt it. A warm feeling passed across her skin. It fluttered around her like thousands of butterflies. Each wing warmed her skin and eased the pain in her body. Her muscles relaxed, and the darkness in her mind ebbed back.

Cassian stopped and helped her down. Grass as soft as velvet stroked her ankles as she passed by. A stream bubbled near them and birds sang the sweetest melodies. Someone sniffled beside her. She wondered what they saw that brought tears to their eyes. The only sights that made her truly cry were the broken bodies of her friends, the other experiments. She cried for them, and with every fiber of her be-ing, she had wished to free them. Even when they used her to bring about their deaths.

Chapter 21

Ot was as if he was dreaming. Cassian walked forward. He couldn't quite control his body, but he wasn't sure he wanted to. The peace that comforted him intoxicated his senses. Cassian wanted to stay there forever. A fog rested against his mind.

Golden light glowed from a giant white oak and illuminated the area they were in. He took his shoes and socks off. The grass felt like a bed with sheets right out of the dryer on it. A warm breeze tickled his nose with the scent of lavender and roses. He choked up from the smell. It smelled like his mother.

A fox skipped in front of the oak tree. It was as black as night with silver eyes. Slowly, it bowed towards Cassian. With a swish of its furry tail, it ran off. He wanted to run after it. A loneliness creeped from the depths of his heart.

"That's the fox from the past couple days," Sebastian said. His speech slurred together as if he was drunk.

Quiet sniffles echoed next to his ear. He whipped around and checked on Leah. Her eyes were clear of tears. She also searched for the sound. Aeron walked across the meadow built within the stone boundaries. A small cobblestone bridge rested above the stream.

Sebastian followed closely behind. His shoulders relaxed and his usual look of weariness dissipated. He looked younger than he was. The hard lines of worry had worn away, and a youthfulness took its place.

The crying grew louder. Cassian held Leah's hand as he investigated. She was quiet as usual, but a little light shone in her eyes. Each step closer to the tree took off a burden from her shoulder, and Cassian's. Everything seemed a little easier there. The fear he had been harboring in the corners of his heart vanished completely alongside the random burst of loneliness.

Leah walked past him, trying to get used to being on her own. Independence was important to her. Cassian knew she was incredibly bothered by her blindness. He thought she was handling it well, but he could see the frustration in her crinkled brows. She shuffled up to the bridge. Her feet barely left the ground and she kicked up dirt and grass.

The crying was loud. Aeron and Sebastian gawked at the tree. Cassian hurried over to them as Leah finished her slowed attempt. She let Cassian bring her over to the tree where the crying was at its loudest. A stone altar sat at the base of the tree. Flowers adorned the sides and moss and vines grew on it. Cries echoed against the stone. Heart wrenching sobs broke loose from the smallest person in the world.

As tall as Cassian's thumb with sheer golden wings, a little fairy bowed at the altar. It mumbled with its head bowed. Sebastian poked Aeron and pointed at it. Aeron backed away from the altar, trying to give it privacy.

Cassian got on his knees and sat beside the small creature. The sobs turned into sniffles. The small fairy turned towards them. Her wings twitched nervously. She curtsied to him. Her eyes landed on Leah, and a sadness washed over her face. The fairy flew up in the air and beckoned them to her tree.

"My head is spinning," Leah said. Her hand gripped Cassian's shoulder as she sat next to him, not seeing the gesture. Her eyelids drooped. She wasn't fully recovered, and the adrenaline of the day wore off. Sebastian checked her temperature as she nodded off. He grimaced, but let her sleep.

"You two go ahead. I'm not interested in the fairy," Aeron said. "I'd feel bad getting into a fight with something so small."

Cassian nodded. Aeron sat next to Leah and let her lean against him. Sebastian raised an inquisitive eyebrow. Cassian laughed at the smirk that Sebastian paired with the look. Aeron's face brightened.

"It is in no way what you're thinking," Aeron said. His face turned red.

Sebastian chuckled and turned away.

"Don't go assuming things." Aeron threw a pebble at Sebastian. He glared at Cassian. "I swear."

"Whatever you do to her, I'll do to you." Cassian gave his sweetest and most innocent smile.

"Go away. You two are annoying."

"I really wouldn't." Cassian laughed. "That would be disgusting, but you know what I mean."

Cassian trotted after Sebastian. The fairy waved to them with a large amount of elegance and grace. She pointed to a door in the tree. It grew in size, going from fairy size to tall Cassian accessible size. It swung open. They cautiously entered the fairy's home.

A large sofa, coffee table, and two rocking chairs welcomed them. The fairy stood on the coffee table which had another set of furniture on it that was her size. Coffee cups floated up towards them. Cassian happily took his. Sebastian eyed the other one before wrapping his hands around it.

"I'm Cassian. I'm sorry to disturb you," he said sheepishly. *What did dad always tell me about fairies?*

She smiled. "I called you so do not be sorry." Her voice sounded like church bells, surprisingly deep and beautiful. "Where are the other two? I noticed the female had shadows in her mind. I thought I could be of assistance."

Sebastian stood. "I'll get them."

She snapped her fingers. "Thank you, Young Sebastian, but I can get them."

Sebastian stared and sat in a rocking chair. Fear and suspicion returned to his face. Cassian sat in the other rocking chair. It was close to a roaring fire. He felt comfortable rather than overheating, as he suspected would happen from sitting that close to the open flames.

The door opened, and the black fox strutted in with a confused Aeron and Leah behind it. Aeron led Leah to the couch and sat next to her, still eyeing the fox. Leah felt the couch. The fibers swayed when she brushed through them. She curled her legs underneath her. Her head leaned against the back of the couch.

"I am Mirabell, the last fairy in this part of the land. My family was kidnapped into the abyss." Mirabell bowed. Her black hair was held tight in a bun, and she wore a beautifully crafted blue dress. "This was my Lord's house. Sadly, He left a long time ago."

"So you live here by yourself?" asked Cassian.

"Yes, I am waiting for the day He comes back. He left on the altar many many years ago." Mirabell's voice cracked. "He sacrificed Himself for our people, but they abandoned Him and got themselves kidnapped."

Aeron leaned forward. Malice swirled in his eyes, and a satisfied smirk played on his lips. "So you want us to save them?"

Mirabell sent a cup of coffee over to Aeron. He refused it. "Yes, Little Aeron, but I will make an exchange. I will save her eyes if you promise to help my people in the abyss. They live in the fourth sector, slaves to a mysterious people group. I will give you an ancient artifact to help you get there."

Sebastian's eyes glowed at the idea of an artifact. He clasped his hands together and leaned back, ready to negotiate for it.

Cassian cleared his throat. "I don't want to be that person, but how much of her eyes can you heal?"

"The most I can do is give her sight back. She'll never be able to see color again though. It seems like the shadows were meant to kill her." Mirabell pouted. "It's the best I can offer. Take it or leave it. You should be lucky she's alive."

Laughter, cruel laughter filled the room. "This is the best you can offer? We face certain death in the abyss to save a people who made foolish mistakes, and you offer us basically nothing? What's an artifact gonna do? Plus, Leah can live without sight until we find someone who will help her without this sketchy stuff going on." Aeron leaned back and threw his arm on the back of the couch. He crossed his legs, making him look like a powerful leader rather than the young guy he was. Cassian shivered. Aeron could be kind of scary. Leah poked Aeron's side. She angrily whispered at him before gazing where Mirabell was.

"There's only one of me here! If my people were here, we'd be able to heal all of you completely." Mirabell sighed. "I can unlock Young

Sebastian's transcendence, on top of all I previously offered. It seems similar to my people's abilities so it should be easy."

"Deal," Leah said. "Heal my eyes."

Mirabell rolled her eyes. "You guys were the best option out of everyone else here, but man, my choice was obviously horrendous."

"See how fast the personality changed," Aeron said. "We shouldn't be making a deal with a fairy at all. And I really hope none of you drank the coffee."

"I'm glad you feel that you can be less formal with us," Cassian said. "I'm also very grateful for you offering to heal Leah's eyes."

"Yeah, yeah," Mirabell said, flying up to Leah's face.

Cassian got up and stood behind the couch. Sebastian followed. Both enamored by the magic that was going to be used to heal Leah's eyes. Mirabell placed her hands on Leah's forehead and began to mumble. A golden light encompassed Mirabell's hands. Her mumbling turned into speaking and then to yelling. Sweat dripped down both Mirabell's and Leah's faces. Mirabell fell and landed on Leah's lap.

Leah blinked and rubbed her eyes. Scooping up Mirabell, her eyes focused on the small creature. Mirabell pat Leah's cheek.

"You have my gratitude," Leah said.

"Don't need it. Just keep your word."

Leah froze, eyes narrowed. She looked up and her jaws dropped. Aeron glanced at her nervously as she concentrated on his face.

"I assumed I would not be able to see any colors."

Cassian scrunched his eyebrows. Confusion and excitement rolled through him. "That's what Mirabell said."

Aeron rubbed his hand through his hair. "Did you finally see how attractive I am?"

"No, but your eyes have color," she said excitedly. "Though I am sorry, Elikar, but we all know I have far superior looks."

Sebastian laughed.

Mirabell tapped her chin and gestured for Sebastian to look at Leah's eyes. Cassian felt useless in the moment. Aeron and Leah were strong fighters. Sebastian took care of their injuries, and Cassian was just there. He watched as Aeron stretched and Sebastian examined Leah. Cassian couldn't do anything like that. He was an okay fighter and a horrible medic.

Am I really needed here?

Mirabell flew up to him and patted his shoulder. "Your feelings are wafting out. They're overwhelming."

Leah slapped Sebastian's hand away. Crossing her arms, she scolded him. He tried to argue back, but his timid nature made it hard. Leah could be bossy.

"Oh, I'm sorry."

"They need you, Cassian. You are their solid ground."

Leah popped up and hugged Cassian as tightly as she could. Mirabell sat on Leah's head, maintaining eye contact with Cassian. Her expression was smug all-knowing. He smiled and hugged Leah back, but gently. She sagged into him. Tears threatened his eyes.

"I was sad not being able to see your face. It is refreshing like a puppy."

Cassian clenched his jaw. "A puppy?"

"You have the eyes." Leah laughed letting him go.

Sebastian reclined in his chair, shoes on the coffee table. He sipped his cup of joe with the eyes of a coffee enthusiast. He savored every sip. "It's a bit rude to tell someone they look like a dog."

Mirabell threw her hands up. "What is with all this useless chattering? If I knew you weren't intelligent, I'd have gone with the elderly man." She slumped her shoulders and glared. "As soon as I'm done with Sebastian, you guys have to leave. I feel you are getting too comfortable in my house."

Chapter 22

irabell kicked them out aggressively to talk to Sebastian, so Cassian, Leah, and Aeron walked in the field. Cassian stopped by the altar and gave a short prayer. He felt morally obligated to do so, even though his family had never been religious.

Leah waited for him at the bridge. Her eyes wandered as she sucked in all the details. She blended in every scenery, and after seeing Mirabell, Cassian confirmed Leah had fairy-like beauty.

Aeron chased the black fox in the grass. It chittered angrily at him, but was appeased when he threw a piece of jerky at it. The fox rubbed itself around Aeron's ankles. Aeron looked around, made eye contact with Cassian, pretended they didn't make eye contact, and picked up the fox. He proceeded to cuddle with it.

"That boy," Leah said with a laugh.

Cassian smiled. "I'm glad you're finally warming up to us."

"It is hard for me." The light in her eyes dimmed. "It will be harder when I am forced to kill one of you."

Cassian gulped. He followed Leah over the bridge. "You don't have to kill anyone."

She turned her head and stared at him over her shoulder. She opened her mouth, but decided against speaking. Leah found his shoes and threw them at him.

Aeron strutted over to Cassian with the black fox wrapped around his neck like a scarf. He walked as if he was a king heading to war—head held high, perfect posture, and the eyes of a beast. The fox nipped at his ear, and Aeron's look of indignity tickled at Cassian. He laughed so hard as Aeron argued with the barking fox. It screamed at him after Aeron insulted its fur.

The fox jumped off of Aeron and ran up to Leah. She picked it up and buried her face in its fur. "You have very nice fur. I am sorry Elikar insults you so."

"What does that even mean?" Aeron attempted to take the fox but Leah trotted behind Cassian.

"Do not worry little dog. Cassian will protect us."

Aeron snorted. "Did you just call it a 'little dog?'"

Leah peeked from behind Cassian. "What are they called then?"

"Foxes," said Cassian. "Or a fox in the case of there being only one."

Leah mumbled in her native language and hid behind Cassian. She sat in the grass with it in her lap. With her hand, she teased the fox's mouth open.

Cassian sat next to her. "I want to pet the little dog too," Cassian whined.

Leah glared at him. Aeron squatted in front of the fox. The fox yipped at him and snapped when he reached to pet it.

He stretched his arms wide. His smile was small. "I'm sorry, alright?"

The fox looked at Leah with big eyes. It licked her cheek apologetically and ran into Aeron. The force of the small animal caused Aeron to fall. He laughed as it licked his face. If Cassian hadn't known better, he'd have assumed Aeron was a normal boy.

Cassian laid in the grass. The holes in the ceiling framed the starry night so he counted the stars. They twinkled in and out of existence, bringing an odd sense of comfort to Cassian while simultaneously making him feel small and even more powerless. Leah flopped on the ground, and Aeron relaxed to her right. The fox snuggled in his lap.

"I wish moments like these lasted forever," Cassian said. A warm breeze lulled his mind and the stars faded out of focus. He shut his eyes.

"If moments lasted forever," Aeron said, his voice far away, "we'd never have any real fun."

Leah snorted. "I assumed you were saying something poetic. I am sorry for assuming too much of you."

"But I'm not wrong. I'd definitely get bored of all these peaceful moments."

"I would rather live a boring peaceful lifestyle than be here," she said quietly.
Cassian rolled over. With her hand outstretched, Leah grasped for a life she couldn't have. The fox jumped out of Aeron's arms and curled up on Leah's chest. It chirped happily.

Sebastian sat in his rocking chair, anticipation making him sweat. He didn't know he had a transcendence. *I can finally be useful.*

"I must warn you," said Mirabell. "This won't be fun. Transcendences are innate powers that are released by intense emotions: bad emotions."

"Wait, what?" Sebastian got out of his chair and headed to the door. "What are you going to do to me?"

Mirabell clapped her hands together, and a long beam of golden light floated in the air. Her expression darkened, and a cruel smile slipped on her lips. With a wave of her tiny hand, the light beam flew at his arm. It went straight through his elbow. Excruciating pain flooded his system, and he screamed. His forearm and hand landed next to him.

"Put it back on," she said.

Sebastian kept sobbing and bleeding out. His head spun from the burning in his arm.

"Put it back on or I'll take the other one off too. You should've never walked into my house, you know." Mirabell laughed. "Now put it back on."

Shaking and light-headed, Sebastian picked up his other arm off the floor. He cried out as it dangled limply in his hand.

"Put it on, Sebastian. Five, four, three—"

Sebastian placed the forearm against his elbow. *Please, please go back on. Please.* A soft gold and silver circle formed around the two pieces. It touched the two pieces of arm, and a cool feeling eased the pain.

"Perfect," Mirabell said.

The arm was completely fine as if nothing happened. Sebastian cradled it. *Does everything that we do have to involve pain?* He opened the door and bawled his eyes out.

Chapter 23

Screaming pierced through the whole ruins with agonized cries following after. Leah covered her ears. Cassian jumped up with Aeron closely behind him. Turning back, Cassian saw Leah curled in a ball. The fox pawed at her and slowly she opened her arms for the fox to crawl into.

The painful shrieking ended abruptly, and Sebastian walked out of the house. The door closed behind him with a slam. He cradled his arm. Cassian saw no physical wounds, but it could be beneath the skin.

Breaking open the door, Aeron forced his way into the house. Lots of glass breaking and crashing accompanied his entrance. Mirabell yelped. Aeron as usual broke out into profanities which, unlike Leah, Cassian thought was funny. Aeron couldn't care less on how people thought of him as long as his point got across.

"What happened? Is there anything I can do for the pain?" asked Cassian. He inspected Sebastian over a second time. He seemed more in shock than in pain.

"She—she lobbed off my arm," Sebastian cried. "She—lobbed it off and forced me to put it back on."

Cassian pitied Mirabell. She had no idea what she caused. Cassian couldn't forgive her for harming Sebastian, but Aeron longed for an excuse to cause chaos.

"If you kill me, your artifact won't be given to you, Little Sefic. AAH!" Mirabell flew through the door. Aeron chased after her. Cassian barely saw Mirabell. She fluttered around the field as a ball of light. "I'll take Leah's eyesight back."

Leah popped her head up and the fox copied her. "I can still kill you blind." It barked in agreement.

"I'm sorry. It had to be done. Transcendence is a curse, not a blessing." Mirabell screeched. "Stop chasing me, boy. I have no interest in anyone other than My Lord."

Aeron stopped and cocked his head. "What're you even saying?"

"You cannot have me." She flew too close to Aeron. With one swoop, he caught her and mercilessly held her by her wings.

The golden ruins flickered into something darker. No animals chirped and the stream was dried. All plant life withered away and the tree twisted into a rotted tangle of branches and roots. Leah and the fox huddled in a sea of dying grass. Cassian shrieked as a white, transparent something floated next to him. On the altar lay a broken body, half decayed and half eaten. As Cassian absorbed the sight and gripped onto Sebastian's arm tightly, the ruins returned to its golden glory.

"If you manhandle me, my magic loosens," Mirabell explained. She struggled in Aeron's loosened grip. He fixed his hand so his fingers wrapped around her torso. "I'm the person keeping this whole island together. How else do you think so many sectors of the abyss are on the surface world?"

Cassian dropped Sebastian's arm and rubbed his hands together. "We're in the abyss?"

"No. Do you fools really not listen? I hate this age group of humans. I am bringing the abyss here. Obviously, I am getting paid." Mirabell smacked at Aeron's hand. "Will you let me go?"

The golden light flickered again. Cassian clasped his hands together and squeezed them until his knuckles turned white. "Why is it so much different?"

Giving up, Mirabell slouched against Aeron's hand. "I projected what it used to be onto what it is now. I don't want to live in such a dismal place for a week. Would you?"

Cassian shook his head fervently. Sebastian walked away from Cassian and joined Leah on the ground across the ruins from Aeron and Cassian. He distanced himself from Mirabell by hiding behind Leah who was significantly shorter than him. The fox rubbed itself on his knee, trying to ease his anxiety, before climbing onto Leah's shoulders and napping.

Mirabell looked at the sky. "It is time for you to go." She forced herself out of Aeron's hand and flew straight to Cassian. Her wings stopped fluttering, and for a moment she was suspended in the air. "Your artifact. I wish you the best on your way out."

A golden light flashed, blinding Cassian, and he saw a compass floating in front of him, right where Mirabell was when the light faded. It was golden on the outside with a fairy engraved on its lid. The fairy had emeralds as eyes. He opened it up and engraved on the underneath of the lid was, *Your heart carries only lies, so instead, follow your eyes.*

The ground rumbled underneath his feet. He caught himself on the tree but it was so rotted his hand went straight through. Her magic dissipated, leaving a stench of rotting and burning. Turning his head to the right, Cassian caught sight of the altar burning. He shoved the compass deep within his pocket.

"That stupid fairy tricked us," Aeron said. He followed Cassian's gaze over to the now reanimated body. The body stretched and jolted in Cassian's direction. It stood on wobbly legs. Pieces of flesh fell as it got its bearings. Cassian ran. He refused to be caught by that.

Aeron shook his head miserably. "It's running."

Stones fell from the roof, landing in a circular pattern. Ghosts fluttered around the stones, reaching their cold fingers towards Cassian as he ran. A dead body and spirits of those long passed chased after him. He counted this as the worst day of his life, but as he ran a foreboding feeling increased. His gut said things were going to get worse. As more stones fell, Cassian prayed that this premonition was all in his head—adrenaline or anxiety.

The fox yowled and ran, dodging the falling stones. It got to the entrance of this room and waited for them. Leah and Aeron followed after it. A stone grazed Aeron's shoulder. Leah grabbed his hand, and pulled him to the other side.

Cassian kept his pace as close to Sebastian's as he could. The entire roof was gone, showing a tunnel that led to the surface. It was impossible to get to. *That would've been so convenient.*

The hallway had also begun to crumble, but the trees and vines held much of it up. Cassian didn't care though. They could buckle at any moment, so Cassian urged the others to keep their pace. They were all growing tired as they ran through what seemed to be a never ending hall.

At last, the fox made a sharp left and Leah let out an excited whoop. They entered into a small corridor with a large wooden door at the back. Windows without glass lined the walls. Plants grew on the floor and walls. She sped up and tried to open it.

She yanked the golden door knob, pushed and pulled the door, rammed her body into its wooden frame. It refused to budge. Cassian pushed against it as well. The body with an entourage of ghosts turned the corner, and Sebastian and the others rammed the door. It did not move an inch.

From the force they exerted, more of the ruin crumbled around them. Panic gripped at Cassian's mind as the crumbling quickened. Piles of stones surrounded them and were building up quickly.

Aeron beat at the door and the fox whimpered. Leah picked the small creature up and jumped out a rusty window beside the door. Cassian gawked before fighting to get his bulky frame through it.

"You left me to die," Cassian yelled as he dropped onto the ground on the other side, rolling on the grass. He didn't get up, laying there absorbing being above the ruins.

Sebastian tumbled out, almost on top of Cassian. He laid flat on the ground. "You should move. Aeron is—"

Aeron pulled himself out of the window and landed on Cassian's leg. He fell from the unstable leg. His head landed on Sebastian's stomach. Sebastian let out a weird noise. "Please, get off."

"Why were you lying right in front of the window anyways?" asked Aeron. He sat up, and Sebastian moved to join Leah who had moved quite a ways away from the ruins.

Cassian got up and looked around. They were back in the forest, but the red beam was closer than ever. They could make it before the deadline if they woke up early in the morning. *I want sleep.*

"Can we stay the night? I'm so tired," said Sebastian.

Cassian looked at Sebastian, gratitude shimmering in his eyes. "Yes, please."

Cassian gathered firewood and placed it in the middle of a rock circle. Leah headed into the forest with the fox at her heel. It barked at her before running deep into the darkness.

Aeron watched them with a look of betrayal. "I was supposed to be the fox's favorite."

"Well ,before you chase after them, please light the fire," Cassian said as he finished setting dried leaves under the wood.

"And now I'm a human lighter! You only saw it one, and you never even complimented me on my cool abilities. The injustice of it all." He snapped his fingers and a tiny flame started at the base of the wood. He spun on his heels and strutted into the forest. "Shrimp, where'd you go?"

Cassian rolled his eyes and dug in his pocket for the compass. "You alright, Sebastian?"

Sebastian nodded. "Well, actually no. That was incredibly traumatizing."

"You've had a rough day," said Cassian. "It's because you're with us. Sorry."

"No!" Sebastian flushed. "I meant I'm good with you guys. All of you make me feel like I'm not a waste of space. It's nice."

Cassian sighed in relief. "Oh good. I don't think we could live much longer without a medic in our group." He flashed a good natured grin. "You're our lucky charm, coming when we needed you most."

Sebastian smiled back, his anxiety clearing up out of his eyes. *I wonder how much longer Sebastian will stay with us. I mean, Leah killed his brother and all.*

"Don't worry. We won't take advantage of you," Cassian clarified.

"I didn't even consider that you would."

"Sebastian, you've got to be mindful of these things. What if you get yourself stuck in a horrible situation because you thought they wouldn't use you." The look of utter disappointment in Cassian's face made Sebastian laugh. "I'm not joking."

"Sorry," Sebastian said through laughs. "You remind me of my mom."

Cassian's face crinkled. "I'm not a mom. If anything, I'm the dad of this group."

"No, you're definitely the mom," Aeron said. His face and clothes were covered in mud. "You don't eat meat right, Baz?"

Leah emerged behind him. A look of triumph settled on her face. She was incredibly clean compared to him. Her arms were full of fish.

"Baz?" asked Leah.

Aeron placed down a bunch of collard greens and lettuce with mushrooms. "Yep. I figured Sebastian was too long."

"I don't mind," Sebastian added.

"Shrimp is longer than Leah," she argued.

"In letters, but not in syllables." The fox sat by Aeron's leg, gazing longingly at the fish. It beggingly barked. "Your cute eyes have no sway over me, not after that betrayal." It barked one last time and ran back to Leah.

Cassian stared at the vegetables. "Where'd you even get these?"

Leah snuggled with it, warming both of them up by the fire. She laughed when Aeron glared over his shoulder at her. "There was a little garden. It was oddly placed, but Aeron thought it was fine to trespass."

Cassian and Sebastian shared an expression. *He's a total goner.* Cassian tried to convey through his eyes. Sebastian nodded.

"I brought fish," Leah said. "It's already cooking."

Sebastian enjoyed the rest of the night. There was lots of chatter and Aeron broke into song. Aeron and Leah argued over the fox's name which Leah won. Nyx barked and ran around excitedly at the birth of a new name.

Aeron held Nyx like a baby and rocked both of them asleep. He slept lightly, waking up briefly at the quietest sounds. Leah watched over them, climbing into a tree for a better view. She waved at Sebastian and Cassian. As she whittled away at a stick, Sebastian let the warm fire lull him to sleep. Cassian followed shortly after, unaware of how loud his snoring was.

Chapter 24

In the early hours of the morning, Nyx snuck out of Aeron's arms, waking him up for a moment before he returned to his light doze. Leah hopped out of the tree and picked up the silky black fox, sneaking away from their makeshift campsite.

The cool morning air nipped at her skin as she headed for the cliff she spotted the night before. Dying leaves crunched under her feet. A chill ran down her spine. The world around her had changed overnight. Even without colors, Leah noticed the death of all the plants in the area. Trees rotted and flowers withered. Nyx growled at a bush and her silver eyes hyper focused on the rustling in the twiggy flora. A large lizard ran out and Nyx barked like a mad dog.

A crunch of leaves alerted Leah of the presence of something or someone else. Nyx quieted and Leah moved out of sight and into the treeline, choosing the thickest and least rotted tree to hide behind. She heard multiple sets of footsteps. One particular creature crashed into multiple trees on its search for her. Nyx pointed her snout in the air and yipped happily.

The fox jumped out of Leah's arms and bolted into the arms of Aeron. The bumbling idiot was in fact her brother. A bruise blossomed on his chin. Sebastian gawked at Cassian as if he didn't know that their "mother" was incredibly clumsy.

"I think we should get out of here," Cassian said, rubbing at his scratch. "Something isn't right?"

"You mean, how everything was bustling with life last night is now dead?" Aeron scratched Nyx under the chin. "Yeah, I agree something is odd."

Sebastian trudged to the cliff's edge. "Look at that sunrise."

The sunlight blinded her for a moment before she let out an exasperated sigh. Her world was exactly how it should be: colorless. The sunrise came in values rather than the majestic and awe-inspiring hues Cassian and Sebastian gushed about. Aeron mirrored her expression. The light reflected off his lilac eyes, the only color she could see.

He smirked when he noticed her staring. "Can't get enough of this?"

"Your eyes are very beautiful." Leah answered honestly. "I could not help but stare. My apologies."

"Oh, I—I wasn't expecting that answer." He laughed, trying to hide his embarrassment. "You can stare at my beauty as long as you like."

"I do not believe you could handle that."

"Leah," Cassian called urgently, "look over there."

Following the line from his finger to the ground, she searched for the cause of his urgency. At the bottom of the cliff was a Lirith garden. Leah knew them well from the one time she visited her father's family. Her grandma had explained that they were once used to adorn places of worship, but now only rich people used them to show their wealth and culture. A small red pavilion with a green roof stood in the middle of the garden with white stones, small streams, and small stone bridges oriented around it. A large crowd of people gathered in front of the structure.

A set of stairs emerged from the side of the cliff. Leah eyed them suspiciously.

Sebastian cleared his throat. "Is today the last day for this trial?"

"Doesn't that mean we passed?" Cassian's eyes lit up.

"We've still got one more trial," said Aeron. "Let's go down, I guess."

They raced down the stairs. Nyx led the group, barking when she thought they were going too slow. Aeron and Cassian raced right behind the fox. Sebastian and Leah jogged after them. Leah was in no rush, and Sebastian needed the slower pace.

She was six steps away from the bottom when a familiar shadow passed her on the cliff face. It almost slipped past Aeron, but the shadow hid its killing intents poorly. Slamming his hand into the wall, Aeron forced his brother out of the wall.

"Do you have anything to say about what happened, Brother?" Aeron sarcastically asked as he bashed his knee in Than's face. He threw him down the rest of the stairs before jumping the rest of them.

Than stumbled back. He tried creating distance between him and Aeron. Aeron rushed forward. He blocked Than's chances of regaining his composure. With a quick movement, Aeron punched his brother in the stomach. Than bent over subconsciously in order to protect his stomach, but his face greeted a knee once again. His nose bent at an odd angle. Blood poured from his nostrils.

"I'm—" Than started before being punched in the jaw. Blood dribbled from his mouth as he spat out a tooth.

He tried counter attacking. However, Than's fighting ability paled in the sight of Aeron's. Than whipped out a knife. Instant regret stiffened his position. Aeron smiled. The predator prepared for his meal. Than trembled.

"If that is how you want to play," Aeron said ecstatically.

In terror, Than lost all reasoning and logic. He swung the blade around. His sides were left unguarded. His fear left him at a horrible disadvantage. Aeron side stepped him, raised his blade, and Leah covered both Cassian and Sebastian's eyes. Aeron stood away from them, cleaning his blades.

"You should not look," she whispered. "For his sake."

"Whose?" Cassian's voice trembled as he asked.

"Aeron's."

"Is this usual for him? Aren't they siblings?" asked Sebastian.

"This is not the first sibling he has had to kill, and unless something changes drastically in his family, it will not be the last." Leah removed her hands from their eyes.

The fight started and ended in mere moments. Cassian closed his eyes and tears streamed down Cassian's face. Leah pitied his sensitive soul, always believing there was good in everyone. She hoped he never learned how wrong that thinking was. All humans were naturally bad, only people like Cassian who had sensitive hearts avoided their evil.

Leah wiped his cheeks, stretching on her toes to reach him. "Who do you cry for?"

"Both of them. Aeron shouldn't have had to do it. He's barely an adult. Why does he have to be forced into a lifestyle like that?"

Aeron stared at Cassian. He moved his lips, but words fell flat.

"Circumstances push us into directions we cannot handle," Leah said kindly. "Aeron has done his best with what he is given. Instead of feeling bad for him, be proud. He has given his all to be able to walk, to live. Don't be happy about his lifestyle, but be proud that he lived it. He could have given it up." The last words came out bitterly.

Cassian avoided looking at the body of Aeron's older brother. Instead, he hugged the three of them, laughing as they all stiffened up like trees. Aeron's face twisted in embarrassment and he protested. Leah slowly wrapped her arms around Cassian and Aeron's waists as she couldn't comfortably reach much higher. Her fingers gripped Sebastian's shirt as that was as far as her short arms could reach. Sebastian wrapped an arm around Cassian's neck and stretched his much longer arms to place a hand on Leah's shoulder. Aeron sighed, before melting into the hug. Leah felt all of them relax.

"I never imagined being able to make my best friends in a week," Cassian said.

Aeron laughed, wiggling out of the hug. Leah imagined his cheeks were flushed a bright red. "We've gone through a lot this week."

"That is an understatement," Leah mumbled. "I have had to be around the two most annoying people in the world and a doctor."

"You better be talking about Cass and Baz." Aeron crossed his arms, grinning.

"Sebastian is a breath of fresh air compared to you."

"I mustn't be that annoying if you haven't stabbed me yet," Aeron whined.

Leah smirked. "We can easily change your misconception."

Nyx let out a whine. She sat patiently outside of their group, waiting for her most deserved affection. Cassian picked her up and Leah patted her head. Nyx yipped happily as they all gave her pets and belly rubs.

A party of four older men around their fifties walked past the young adults. The leader was a small man with strawberry blond hair and a long nose. He was joined by a tall and muscular black man, a woman with sharp eyes and a predatory smile, and a short weasley guy whose prideful gait irritated Leah. Judgment lingered on their faces, and Leah knew they were deciding who would be the easiest prey. Obviously it was Aeron, but their eyes stayed on her. Indignation flared through Leah but she ignored it. They were not worth her time. For she had little of it.

Cassian led the group of young adults with a screaming Nyx in his arms to the pavilion. He trotted happily to the steps. A woman brushed shoulders with him, sizing Cassian up. Nyx bit her hand. The woman shrieked as corrosion from Nyx's bite spread from her palm to her elbow. Nyx chittered at the woman angrily, curling up into a ball in Cassian's arm.

"Is Nyx the reason why the forest died?" Sebastian asked. "Did we take her from that sector of the abyss?"

Leah stood in front of Cassian and Nyx. "Are you going to make us get rid of her?"

Sebastian shook his head. "I like Nyx just as much as you."

Leah relaxed until she heard the creaking of metal. The bottom of the pavilion opened up and a large platform rose from the ground. Her uncle stood on the platform, his arms spread wide in his usual theatrics.

Chapter 25

"**C**ongratulations on passing the second trial. I fear there are too many of you. We only require ten attendees. I apologize to those who don't make it," the man, who Leah obviously hated, said. Aeron understood why. He was annoying and so dramatic. Aeron was shocked by the resemblance Leah and the man had: same nose and chin, similar eye color. It freaked Aeron out a little.

Twenty men dressed in green camouflage with large rifles strapped onto their backs appeared out of nowhere and stood in a line. They stood as straight as a ruler, breathing in-sync. Leah's enemy shouted over the murmuring. Leah flinched next to Aeron. All men readied their weapons in the same motion. They cocked their guns at the same time and waited for the final command.

Leah pulled Baz to the ground and Aeron did the same with Cassian. In mere moments, a third of the contestants laid on the ground in their own blood. Seeking refuge, Aeron and Cassian crawled away from the pavilion. They lost sight of Leah and Sebastian. Nyx slunked besides Aeron, growling quietly. As soon as Aeron thought they were out of firing range, they ran back to the cliff face. The stairs were nowhere in sight.

Aeron could take most of those men with little difficulty. He'd possibly get hurt but he would live. Sebastian's head popped over the frenzied mass. A bullet embedded itself in the brains of the person next to him. He ducked down.

"Should we help them?" asked Cassian.

Sitting against the cliff face, Aeron stifled his frustration. "We'd only get in the way. Leah already has to worry about Baz."

Cass wore a path as he paced back and forth. Seconds turned into minutes. Bodies adorned the garden and blood stained the white stones. The soldiers separated from their line. A group of older men faced the soldiers head on. One by one, men and women fell, reluctantly meeting their maker.

Pink hair glittered in the early afternoon sun. Baz walked by her side, keeping an eye behind them. She stalked over to them. Each step conveyed her rage. Baz was pristine aside from the build up of dirt and grime from days without proper bathing, while blood covered Leah's hands and knife.

"I see it went well," Aeron said, meeting them in the middle.

"Well? Leah killed like four people." Sebastian turned around and hunched over. His stomach contents fertilized the weeds.

Leah changed into something else. With incredibly straight posture and stiff movement, if she wore their green uniform, she'd have blended in as a soldier. Her presence was intimidating. Cass wiped blood off her cheek. She slapped his hand. With one look at her face, he backed off. Her bloodlust included anyone who annoyed her.

"Back down, Shrimp," commanded Aeron. "He's trying to help."

"You are not my commanding officer. I take no orders from you."

Anger flared in his mind. "That doesn't mean you treat your friends rudely."

"What would you know about friends? You were a sheltered kid. You only knew your parents and like three of your siblings."

"You two need to stop," Cassian jumped in. Baz flinched. He backed away from the rising voices and angry tones. Nyx joined him on the sidelines. She slid her tail between her legs and whimpered.

"It isn't like you had friends either. You were locked away for most of your life." Aeron instantly regretted his words. Leah looked up at him with disinterest.

"You are right. How kind of you to pour salt in my festering wounds." Leah spoke in a monotone voice. "At least, I had friends, but they are dead now. I killed them. I killed them. They made me kill them. I had absolutely no control of my body, and they used me. They could not handle the rape and torture they went through so they made me remove them from their misery. Every last one of them. But no one will end my misery." She wiped her face as tears streamed uncontrollably from her eyes. "Dang you Elikar. You always make me cry."

Aeron's temper cooled. "Sorry. I should've been a bit more sensitive."

"A bit?" Baz said sarcastically.

Leah looked up, rubbing away any remnants of tears. "I am tired of having everyone ripped away from me by him."

"Do you think he could get us?" Cass asked. A few last gunshots cracked in the air behind them.

Her shoulders shook with emotion. Aeron knew besides her episode a few days ago, Leah showed her emotions very rarely. She couldn't handle them by herself. And as she sobbed, Aeron would've done anything to make her smile.

Cass hugged her and she wept bitterly on his shoulder. She apologized in his shirt, soft and heartfelt apologies.

Baz eyed the pavilion. "I think everything's cleared up, but I'm not comfortable going back."

Still sniffling, Leah stepped away from Cass. "I agree. I do not want to go back."

"We'll just hang out here until they call for us," Aeron said.

Things never go as planned for the quartet though, so Aeron shouldn't have been surprised when a blue tube of light surrounded Leah. Her eyes widened and she smacked at the sides of it. Cass moved towards her when another tube formed around him. He stayed calm, unlike Leah who was still bashing her hands on the tube. Blood dripped down them as she cracked her skin over and over again. Baz grabbed Nyx as the tube around him formed.

The three of them disappeared. Aeron swiveled around, coming face to face with Leah's enemy. "You seem promising." The man cackled. Aeron jumped back, pulling out his knife. "I won't harm you, Boy. Besides, your father will kill me if I take you now." A blue tube formed around Aeron and the man pressed his face against it. "If you continue ruining my precious Jin-Ae, I will end you no matter what the consequences. I need her."

Light flooded Aeron's vision and his stomach twisted. The force of being teleported didn't sit well with the small breakfast he ate. His head spun as the speed increased.

Chapter 26

Leah collapsed onto cold hard metal. She looked around wildly for any of the boys. She was alone in a pitch black room. Hands grabbed her shoulders and shoved her to the ground, slamming her head against the flooring. Leah kicked at her assailants like a horse, putting as much of her waning strength into her legs. She made contact with a knee.

A man swore and let her go, leaving another set of hands pinning her down. Thrashing and kicking, she attempted to hit the other assailant. Lights flashed on and a white lab coat fell in her face. A needle sunk into her skin. Her body went numb and she lost feeling in her limbs. The men dragged her across the floor by her hair. Pain seared in her scalp.

Cassian stood on the other side of a pane of thick soundproof glass. The party of midlife crisis individuals who'd sized her up an hour before, held Cassian and Aeron back. Nyx pawed at the glass. Her claws left black scratch marks. The black man held Aeron against the wall, and the woman rested a knife against Sebastian's throat. The Weasley guy tripped Cassian and stepped on his back. Sebastian's throat bobbed as he gulped.

This wasn't what she was expecting for the last test. She fought as two large men in pearly white lab coats put on a straight jacket. She could smell the antiseptic on their clothes. Leah's mind went blank. All her natural and unnatural instincts died away. It took every ounce of her concentration to keep her breathing stable.

Eyes were on her as they dragged her across the white room with metal floors. Metal floors were easier to clean when the doctors got blood on it. An upright metal table with metal straps was placed directly in the middle of the room. A whimper slipped from her mouth. She lifted her head slightly, hoping to see a familiar face. The old people stood in her way. Nyx pressed her face against the glass. Leah let go of some of the stress. She wasn't fully alone.

They lifted her limp body. Her arms dangled as they placed her on a metal table. The cold emanating from it caused the shivering to almost become convulsions. Thick leather straps latched onto her limbs and midsection. The two men backed away and out of the room as he walked in. He strutted behind her, caressing her cheek. His smile was warm and caring on the surface, but Leah knew what he was waiting for. He placed wires and monitors on her arms, legs, stomach, and chest. She shook uncontrollably.

"I've missed you. None of my new test subjects have performed as well as you have. The numbers don't impress anymore." His voice, rich and deep, echoed in the silence. He looked just like her mother, tall with beautiful brown skin. Curly hair fell into his chocolate brown eyes. She didn't need color to remember what he looked like. He never changed. A familiar crooked grin caused longing in Leah. She wanted her mother—the one who shared that grin. "I'm very disappointed in you. I gave you one job: to obey, and you do the complete opposite. How does it feel to have the blood of your friends on your hands?"

Looking directly at the window, Leah whispered, "Please, someone save me."

Cassian headbutted his assailant. They were trying to get her, trying to save her. Over Aeron's head was a large fireball. Even Sebastian struggled to get to her.

"My dearest niece, do you believe you're even worth saving? You're dumber than I remember. Maybe a little reminder will toughen you up." He snapped his fingers.

That's when it started. The burning that is. "I beg of you," she said through screams. "Anything but this."

Her body heated up and burned from the inside out as the electric currents ran through her body. The man laughed, joining in with her screaming. Shock after shock, he burned the moment into her memory. Over and over again, he punished her. Just as he had done when she was young and naive. It first happened when she bit his assistant, but it became more common. All the times she protected her companions, her sisters, he would give all of them a "special treat" as he called it.

"Jin-Ae, this is for your good." His ecstatic smile said otherwise. "You'll unlock your transcendence and be useful. Our testing has proven that trauma unlocks a string of DNA. The DNA controls magic use. Doesn't that make you excited? You're going to show everyone here how well our testing works. This is getting boring though. Why don't we spice things up?"

"No! No more. I'm sorry," Leah cried between ragged screams.

Blue strips pulsed from the electricity. Fear, pain, and hatred blurred her vision. The voltage increased and Leah's heart couldn't take the amount of electricity. After one last high voltage hit, her heart stopped beating. Everything stopped. Blood stopped pumping through her veins, oxygen didn't fill her lungs, and her brain stopped functioning.

She failed Alayna again. She always failed them.

Her heart monitor flatlined. The machine's screaming echoed around the room, bouncing off the walls. Cassian's heart plummeted. He needed to save her. With as much strength as he could muster, Cassian forced himself off the ground. The man who pinned him down yelped as Cassian threw off his balance. Cassian stood up as fast as he could.

"Don't move, or we kill these two," the leader said. His presence was calm. Wrinkles formed under his grey eyes.

The black man jumped away from Aeron. Aeron set himself on fire, and the smell of burning fabric filled the room. "You'd probably only kill Baz, but Nyx got to you first."

A knife clattered to the floor. Corrosion and decay spread up the woman's body like poison in her bloodstream. Nyx chittered angrily as Sebastian collapsed on the ground in relief. Aeron sent a ball of crackling fire hurling towards his previous captor.

"I can handle this," Aeron said. "You two go save our Shrimp."

Cassian ran to the window and beat his hands on the glass above Nyx's corrosion marks. The sides of his hands stung as blood dripped down the window. The man in the lab coat took the monitors and wires off Leah. The monitors quieted. The man grabbed her head and moved it around. It flopped limply. She wasn't moving, breathing. Her eyes, though open, didn't twinkle with life.

Sebastian ran to the door and jiggled the handle. He jumped back. "Too much electricity was charged up in the room. I can't grab the handle."

A fiery hand slammed against the glass, melting a fist sized hole in the glass. Aeron put his other hand in the hole and melted it even more. Cassian snapped, trying to figure out how Aeron summoned his transcendence. He felt power surge from his core. It traveled down his arm and water bubbled at his fingertip. He pulled more magic out, shaping it into a large drill. With all his anger, Cassian pierced the glass. Shards flew at his face and arm, cutting his skin.

The man did a little bow after turning towards the clean window. Obviously aware that his audience couldn't help but watch. "Don't worry fellows, we have only just started the show."

A hand grabbed Cassian's shoulder. Before he reacted, Aeron punched the individual with his hand ablaze. Fire casted long dark shadows on his face. The rage and bloodlust matched Cassian's. Cassian never wanted to hurt anyone, but at the moment if the man torturing Leah died, he hoped it would be in the most dreadful way possible.

Window shards crashed to the ground with enough space for the boys to enter the torture chamber one by one. Aeron entered the room first. He charged after the man as Cassian ran to Leah. The room was much larger than he expected. Nyx guarded the exit while Sebastian joined Cassian at Leah's side.

Sebastian pressed his index and pointer fingers against her neck. He moved them around, searching desperately for a pulse. He dropped his hand to his side and turned to Cassian. Cassian swallowed back tears and brushed Leah's hair off of her face. He held her hand, pressing her chilling hands to his forehead.

Beep. Beep. She wasn't connected to the heart monitor. One after another, it beeped becoming more and more steady. The lights flickered in the room. A current of electricity blasted through one of the lightbulbs. Cassian watched it wrap around Leah's arm.

Felix and the elderly Lady Elizabeth ran into the room. Felix looked around the area with a bewildered expression. Aeron truly took care of the party. The only one left breathing was the leader who sat against the wall with a completely destroyed leg. Cassian met his grey eyes. No anger or resentment showed in them. Instead, he watched the event with contentment. Lady Elizabeth slowly made her way to the glass opening. Nyx barked and bowed before letting the Lady in.

A stray electric bolt shattered the remainder of the window. She shook off his hand. Sebastian tore off the straps and Leah sat up stretching. With an elegant movement, She swung her legs off the bed. Electricity trailed down her skin and left burn marks on the floor. Leah walked towards Aeron. Her eyes focused on the man he attempted to fight.

"Let us end this, Alejandro," she said.

Felix ran in. "Jin-Ae, no!"

Aeron backed away. His eyes followed her every movement. Leah physically lived, but emotionally she died. Her dark eyes swirled with fear, anxiety, and a thirst for revenge. A ball of electricity sat in the palm of Leah's hand. She walked up to Alejandro, the electricity getting excited.

"I wouldn't if I were you," he said. "The moment I die, so does Alayna."

Leah's face twisted with hatred and disgust. The electricity died down. Cassian and Sebastian ran to her side. Concern ate away at Cassian.

"I know where she is," Alejandro stated confidently. "Now, it's a race to see who gets there first: me or you."

Sebastian snorted. "Oh, really? Is that why you need Leah?" He spoke with more confidence than Cassian had ever heard. Aeron was beginning to rub off on him. Cassian considered the thought for a second; He actually rubbed off on everyone for better or worse.

Alejandro growled like a dog and lunged forward, pulling out a vial from his pocket. As he tossed it, Aeron punched him in the nose. Alejandro stumbled back in shock and pain. Aeron gave him a smug look and Alejandro's face darkened. "You fool of a Sefic, don't think this is the end of me. We have already discussed the consequences.."

Alejandro threw down a white stone. Aeron backed off as a large portal opened, sucking in the air. Leah's hair flew in front of her towards the portal. Alejandro threw his vial at her. There was no time for her to dodge.

With the presence of royalty, Lady Elizabeth stepped in front of Leah while Cassian shielded his sister. The liquid melted her clothes, revealing metal armor. The table in the room hovered. It twisted and floated in circles. Madam Elizabeth raised a wobbly hand and the table flew into the portal, disrupting it.

"If you know what's in your best interest, Jin-Ae, you'll come back to me. I'm willing to spare those friends of yours if you want. I will get what I want even if you never control yourself again. You and everything else in this world belong to me."

Madam Elizabeth placed both hands on her cane. "I had heard the rumors, but the council requested that you administer one of the trials. Your knowledge is extensive, but you have let greed corrupt your mind. I will report you to the council and have your license revoked."

"Unlike you fools, I don't need a license. I have what the leaders want and I will get what I want in return."

He stepped into the unstable portal, and it closed behind him. He was gone before Cassian could process what Lady Elizabeth said. Cassian moved away from Leah and let Sebastian examine her. She stood incredibly still as he poked and prodded at her arms. He checked her pulse and eyes.

There was no physical injury—no bruising or scarring, and no signs of internal injury. A different type of injury formed. The wounds on her heart had reopened, and she was completely lost in her head. Aeron carefully dragged her out of the room. He sat her on the floor and talked to her about anything and everything as Felix and Lady Elizabeth worked with the rest of the attendees. They scanned Cassian, Aeron, and Sebastian over with an odd glowing orb.

Felix looked as if his heart had been ripped into two when he saw Leah sitting there. Her eyes were vacant and lifeless. Cassian felt the expression Felix gave Leah on an emotional level. Though Aeron acted as if he knew how to help her. Cassian prayed to anything that would listen, asking that Leah would be able to overcome the reliving of her nightmares.

The elderly gentleman dragged him and his ruined leg over to them. Aeron put a fiery arm in front of Leah, protecting her from the mastermind. He whacked Aeron in the head. "I can bring her some comfort."

Aeron looked at Sebastian who shrugged. "Make one suspicious move and I'll kill you. Leaving you alive was a mercy because I thought you'd be interesting. Don't make me regret it."

"You are possessive but understood," the old man said. He pressed his wrinkly hands against Leah's forehead. She looked up at him with disinterest. With a sharp light, she leaned her head against Cassian's leg and fell into a deep sleep. "She will sleep until you call her true name."

As the other trial runners began to leave the room, Cassian moved Leah's head off his leg and stood up. Nyx tried to crawl into her lap. Gently, he picked Leah up and carried her, following behind Sebastian and Aeron.

Chapter 27

"Jin-Ae," Cassian said.

With sleep in her voice, Leah groaned. "Don't call me that."

"Sorry."

They were in the room they had started the blasted trials in. Any blood had been cleaned off the floor, and the carcasses of those who had died were nowhere to be seen. Leah was relieved. She was too nauseous to deal with that type of carnage at the moment.

Leah forced herself onto her feet. A crowd of people gathered around Felix and Lady Elizabeth. Leah's head pounded and static ran through her clothes. Brushing against Sebastian, she shocked him.

Leah rubbed sleep out of her eyes. Aeron, Cassian, and Sebastian walked in front of her, shielding her from the other attendees. Cassian continually looked back at her. Despite having slept for a good while, she was exhausted. The old man hobbled alongside her. His light eyes were warm, and she scraped her original judgment of him. Was he calculating behind his calm? Yes, but she appreciated his calm.

Besides the four of them and the old man, there was one large lady with her hair in a thick braid and a war hammer, a calculating young man with guns and fur strapped all over his body, and a middle aged man with a scar across his face. Lady Elizabeth walked into the center of the room. Her shoulders slumped.

Cassian linked their arms together, and Leah stared up at him. He patted her hand while Sebastian ruffled her hair. The elderly man leaned against Aeron, who furrowed his brows at the trusting gesture. Aeron smirked at Leah who returned with a small smile. His eyes glistened with color.

Lady Elizabeth bowed her head low. "You have my humblest apologies for Professor Perez's actions. While we expected many of you to die and be in immense pain, it was not to be directly given by an administrator. Evidence has been found of his illegal actions, and the council of the trials will be dealing with it shortly. He was never to be a Trial Master in the first place. He paid his way into the position."

The wall opened up and revealed a wooden table. Felix walked over and picked up a stack of golden cards. He beckoned to the Trial Runners. Leah and Cassian walked up confidently with Sebastian behind them. Aeron hobbled over slowly because despite his best efforts, he could not get rid of the old man. Leah wondered if his guilt prevented him from taking any forceful action against the man.

With a smile, Felix handed each of the attendees their license. Cassian thanked him for both of them. It was made of gold plated steel. A treasure chest in the middle of a compass was etched on the back.

"Once you have your license, please go over to the orb we scanned you with that is over at the end of the hall. We will meet you at the end of the stairs." Lady Elizabeth walked out of the room.

Felix ran up to Leah and crushed her in a hug. Her back popped. "You made it! You did a great job. When you get to the third layer, you'll have to visit me. Promise?"

Leah smiled and he frowned. "You know..."

"I know," he agreed. His eyes drooped. "I just—I don't want to go through what happened with Mel again." He forced a smile. "Gotta go. Be safe and rethink it. If not for my sake, then theirs."

Cassian and Aeron ganged up on Sebastian. Cassian slapped the poor guy's shoulder and Aeron jumped on his back. He rolled his eyes and refused to move. Aeron got bored and harassed Cassian instead ran away, laughing. The elderly gentleman was long gone. Nyx chased them, nipping at their ankles. Sebastian ran away from the barking fox.

"Nyx, don't you dare! I don't know how to take care of necrosis. No. Nyx." Sebastian ran past Leah. "Tell your pet to stop."

A smiling Felix left Leah to ponder over his plea. Cassian tripped over Sebastian's foot and Leah raised a brow. She tucked the words deep in her heart next to the box filled with her emotions.

"Ready to go, Shrimp?" Aeron said as he tackled Sebastian to the ground.

Leah strutted to the door. "That is an understatement. The more I watch, the less I want to be around."

She swung open the door. The hallway was lined on every wall with doors, and an orb flaoted at the top of a stairwell. Leah headed over to it. Her footsteps and the footsteps of the horseplaying boys resounded around them. The orb spun around and bounced up and down. A paper hung on the wall next to it.

To personalize your license, place your card in the orb and state your name.

The orb absorbed her card. "Leah... Leah Kimura." It flashed green and a picture of her projected on its side. *Does this picture work? Yes or no.* "Yes." It spat out her card.

Her name was at the top beside a magically generated picture of her. Underneath her name, her birthday, general physical features, and birth country were listed. An empty spot labeled "sectors" showed how little of the abyss she'd explored as an adventurer.

With a sigh, she headed down the stairs. The boys called for her to wait, but she was so close to reaching Alayna that she tuned everything out.

Chapter 28

The stairs descended for what seemed like eternity and with each step, Cassian feared this would be the last time he saw his friends—his best friends. Sebastian trotted down the stairs, sweat running down his face, and his breath coming out in quick puffs. Nyx ran past him and threw herself down at Aeron. He laughed when she landed on his neck. Barking loudly, Nyx alerted everyone of her happiness.

Leah stopped half way down. She leaned against the wall and waited for them. They picked up the pace and passed her one by one. Nyx jumped off Aeron and into Leah's arm, gaining a glare from Aeron which she received with a small smile. In order to catch his breath, Sebastian stopped on the step above her and leaned against the wall.

When Cassian passed her, she started descending again. Sebastian walked with her and Aeron slowed down so they could walk as a group.

"This is it, isn't it?" asked Cassian. His voice cracked. "Oh, that's embarrassing." Silence followed suit and the lack of an answer hurt. "That's a dumb question."

"I don't want this to be the end," said Sebastian. His voice was barely a whisper.

Aeron smirked at them. "I know I'm so charming, but you guys don't have to be so desperate."

"No one is desperate for you, Elikar." Leah cuddled Nyx. "Even Nyx only finds you tolerable."

He huffed and skipped down the steps. "You're insufferable."

The end drew closer. A breeze blew through the tunnel. Cassian enjoyed the wind as it cleared the stuffiness of the stairwell. It smelled of flowers and fresh rain.

"For at least the first sector, would you guys like to be a party until we establish ourselves?" asked Leah. Her voice raised an octave. "It only has to be until we settle ourselves into a guild."

Cassian broke out into a huge grin. Reaching the end of the stairs, he ran out excitedly and faced them. "What should we call our party?"

No one answered. Each of them focused on something behind him. Slightly embarrassed, he turned around. Thousands of miles wide and infinitely deep, the abyss laid before them. Large air lifts spanning miles long hung to the side of the abyss. The abyss was completely outside. People set up shops and tourist attractions along the rim. Many people who go on residency licenses could hire bodyguards and mercenaries to protect them all the way down to the third sector. Only adventurers could travel past that.

His heart pounded in his chest. This was it. He was finally following in his dad's footsteps. Cassian would finish his dad's dream for him, and find who took that dream away from him.

"Cassian!" A familiar voice called to him. She in her fullness ran over to him and squeezed the living daylights out of him. "My baby! You made it."

He hugged his mom. "I missed you."

"You stupid boy." She hit him in the back of his head, tears in her eyes. "I should've thrown away those letters. My heart failed multiple times. The videos they posted were horrible." She turned to Leah and Aeorn. "You two are in big trouble. Fighting within your group is going to get you killed."

Aeron rubbed the back of his head and Leah looked away sheepishly. Amyra hugged both of them. "I'm so proud of both of you," she whispered to them. Finally, she got to Sebastian who stood awkwardly with his hands folded in front of him. She squeezed the breath out of him. "Thanks for helping these dummies along. Now, follow me. Let's get you washed up and fed."

Amyra led them to a fancy hotel on the rim of the abyss. Leah and Amyra shared a room, and Cassian and the others shared a room. They said a quick farewell at the women's room where Amyra gave them a fresh set of clothes with a promise of a nice warm dinner in two hours.

"I call first dibs on the shower," said Aeron, running through the hall with his key card.

Cassian sighed. "That's not fair."

"I want to shower too," said Sebastian.

"Well you'll have to wait." Aeron unlocked the door and rushed into the bathroom. "I plan to take a super long shower."

To Cassian and Sebastian's dismay, he did.

Leah sat with Amyra at the dining table they'd reserved at a very nice restaurant. This dinner was Amyra's gift for making it through the trials. They were still waiting on the boys who were ten minutes late already.

"Leah," Amyra said. "When you're in the abyss, please look after Cassian."

Before Leah could reply, Aeron threw open the restaurant's door. He wore a light button down and slacks. His hair was ruffled in a very meticulous way. Cassian and Sebastian followed behind him. They were going off on the arrogant assassin.

"You took an hour-long shower," said Sebastian. "That's ridiculous when you knew we wanted to shower too."

"You two were sleeping when I got out." Aeron laughed.

"Because you were taking forever." Cassian looked as if he wanted to rip Aeron's head off.

Aeron sat next to Leah, giving her a small smile. "You look so much better than before."

Leah glared at him. "And you smell bearable."

Cassian chuckled. "You should've seen how much cologne he sprayed in our room."

"It was like he was trying to impress someone, but now I smell disgusting too," Sebastian said.

Leah laughed. The food was brought out in large quantities, and while Cassian still had to take a bit of each item, Leah ate wholeheartedly. Amyra told stories about Wesson and his crew, soft music played in the background, and everyone was laughing and cheering. Her mind would wander from the conversation, but one of her friends would always bring her back. They were watching her, and she watched them.

It is nice to have people to belong to. I hope Alayna loves them too.

Chapter 29

Amyra put her hands on her hips. "Now off you go. Take care and send me letters from wherever you can. You won't be able to make it to the abyss this afternoon if you don't leave now."

She pulled off her backpack and handed it to Sebastian. "I brought tons of medical supplies. You're definitely going to need them. Apparently those two—" She looked directly at Aeron and Leah—"cannot keep themselves safe to save their lives. I'm truly sorry for all the trouble they will cause."

Giving everyone one last hug, the whirlwind of a mother left. Cassian's heart broke as his mom joined the crowd of spectators who watched the new and old adventurers and residents alike take off down into the world of wonder and despair. Excitement ran through the crowd.

"Last call for departure!" The host motioned people to board an air lift.

The four of them booked it. They weaved through a crowd of people, ducking under arms and around living obstacles. Aeron let out a holler and jumped in the air as he entered into the air lift first, showing the host his license. Sebastian and Leah hopped in next.

"Cassian!" they all yelled for him.

He sped up and into the lift while the host closed the door. His golden license reflected in the host's eyes, and he nodded his approval. Cassian quickly found a seat saved by his friends. Aeron flashed him a grin. "What about The Quartet?" asked Leah.

"For what?" Cassian questioned, settling into his seat. He pulled out the compass and opened it. The needle pointed down. He realized that the compass didn't have the cardinal directions in it. It just pointed down.

"Our party's name. We'll have to have one so the guild knows we are working as a team."

Aeron frowned. "That's lame. At least add some sort of adjective."

"But we wouldn't be mistaken for anything else than the four of us," Sebastian added. His eyes brightened. The backpack contents spilled out on the floor. Piles of bandages, gauze, and disinfectant sat on his lap. He happily inspected all the medicines and ointments Amyra had packed.

"At least add 'magnificent' or something," Aeron whined.

"We could be Nyx's Quartet," Sebastian added. Nyx barked and wagged her tail, earning a pet from him.

"Nyx approves, so I'll approve too," Aeron said.

Wind rocked the lift. Cassian turned his gaze outside. Rock walls shot up down far beyond the eyes could see. Small plants grew in little outlets, and a giant bird flew by the window. It was as big as a dragon, with a sharp beak and feathers as red and yellow as the sky at sunset. A large black eye peered in before it flew down into the abyss.

A city came into view, the first city in the sector, and where the main guild halls resided. Leah pressed her head against the window, watching as hundreds of buildings grew closer. A look of dread and uncertainty lingered on the faces of everyone in the lift.

What does the future hold? Cassian wondered. He was excited, but the same dread filled him. *Would it be worth it all?* He didn't know if all the lives lost were worth treasure and glory. As long as he could find out what really happened to his dad, Cassian didn't care which scared him.

The golden watch glowed and grew hot. Cassian dropped it out of his hand, but it suspended in the air. Leah eyed it and scooted away. A bright light illuminated the whole car, and people began to stare and grow anxious around them. The glowing stopped and the compass was gone. In its place, Mirabell flapped her wings.

"Missed me? Can't have you forget your promise, can I?"

Acknowledgments

There are so many people that I have to thank for this book. First off, everything I do is for my Savior, and I hope that my writing and the messages I weave into this story are honoring and pleasing to Him. Next would be my wonderful family has not only been encouraging, but also very supportive which has been such a blessing. Mimi also did a ton of the art for the series which everyone should be grateful for since she brought the characters to life for me.

Following those two groups would be all of my friends, irl and online. Betsy and Ry, you have seen this at its worst, and I beg of you, please forget it. I've done my best to make it significantly better. Liv, you inspired a bit of Leah's personality, and I feel a bit bad. I would never have gotten this far in WYRIA without Lucy who is such an inspiration to me and has become one of my closest friends. Violet, Ser, and Susan, your words have meant the world to me and have helped calm my anxiety so many times.

Lastly, I would like to thank my beta team and my street team. This garbage is only less garbage because of the wonderful people on my beta team who literally tore this apart in the nicest ways possible. My street team has put a lot of work into helping me market and promote this as well as just being an encouragement. I am forever in all of your debts.

About the Author

From a young age, Lorelei R. Jensen has adored books. Reading with a flashlight late into the night wasn't uncommon for her at all. She wrote off and on during elementary school, but it wasn't until she got hold of her first self-published book that she decided she wanted to be an author. Currently, she lives with her parents and younger sister in the hot and dry desert of Arizona.

www.ingramcontent.com/pod-product-compliance
Lightning Source LLC
Chambersburg PA
CBHW060407310726
48976CB00003B/967